MATTHEW SWANSON & ROBBI BEHR

the Real McCoys

TWO'S a CROWD

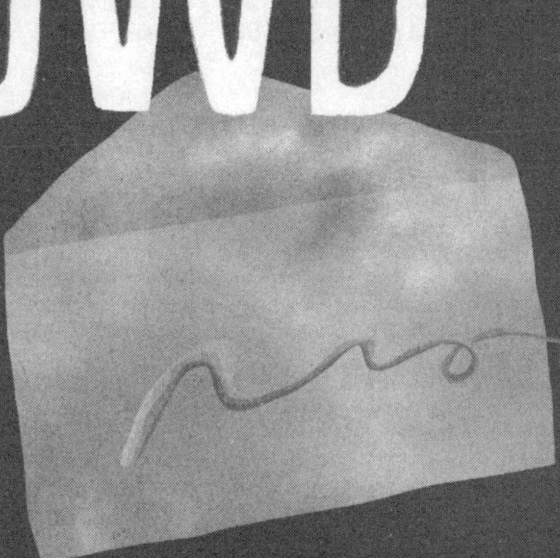

[Imprint]
MAKE YOUR MARK

NEW YORK

To Clifford, for setting the table.
To Robin, for bringing the light.

[Imprint]
MAKE YOUR MARK

SQUARE
FISH

An imprint of Macmillan Publishing Group, LLC
120 Broadway, New York, NY 10271
mackids.com

Our books may be purchased in bulk for promotional, educational, or business use. Please
contact your local bookseller or the Macmillan Corporate and Premium Sales Department at
(800) 221-7945 ext. 5442 or by email at MacmillanSpecialMarkets@macmillan.com.

ISBN 978-1-250-09857-3 (paperback) / ISBN 978-1-250-23249-6 (ebook)

Originally published in the United States by Imprint
First Square Fish edition, 2019
Book designed by Natalie C. Sousa
Imprint logo designed by Amanda Spielman
Square Fish logo designed by Filomena Tuosto

10 9 8 7 6 5 4 3 2 1

AR: 4.6 / LEXILE: 670L

This book is a letter from me, meant for you.
My message is simple. My motives are true.
Once you digest it, do share what you've learned.
And if you have borrowed, please read then return.
Or else, on my honor, with Milton as proxy,
I'll have to unleash the full fury of Moxie.

CHAPTER 1: THE SECRET HANDSHAKE

"The name's Moxie. Moxie McCoy."

You may know me by my deeds, which are legendary. You might be startled by my speed and smarts and lightning-quick reflexes, which are, quite frankly, unrivaled. You probably haven't heard of my puny little brother, Milton, but here he is, stuck to my side, like a leprechaun chasing a rainbow.

To the untrained eye, it might look like we're walking to school, but we are, in fact, working. On the lookout for peril, mishap, and disaster. Ready to save the world at a moment's notice.

MY hero and mentor, Annabelle Adams, Girl Detective, is only twelve years old, but she has saved the world 58 times already, once for each book in her series, which I have read 39¾ times and can recite to you from memory with one hand tied behind my back and the other one eating an apple.

I'M ALL HEART!

After saving our school and solving the crime of the century, Milton and I are in search of a bigger, trickier, more death-defying challenge.

But for days and weeks, the world has been boringly normal. No capers! No heists!

NOT EVEN A MISSING LUNCH BOX!!!

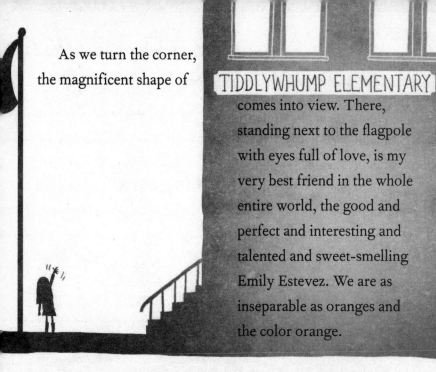

As we turn the corner, the magnificent shape of **TIDDLYWHUMP ELEMENTARY** comes into view. There, standing next to the flagpole with eyes full of love, is my very best friend in the whole entire world, the good and perfect and interesting and talented and sweet-smelling Emily Estevez. We are as inseparable as oranges and the color orange.

I have not talked to Emily for *three whole days* because she has been camping with her family in a cabin that does not have a phone.

Emily!

Moxie!

We face each other, stick out our elbows, and do the most intricate-and-difficult-to-learn-or-duplicate secret handshake in the history of best-friendship.

3

Its many moves include "dump the soup," "love the slug," and "chop the avocado," because, as everyone knows but so few are willing to admit, soup is awful, slugs are incredibly lovable, and guacamole is the world's most perfect appetizer.

Secret Handshake

TAP THE ELBOWS

DUMP THE SOUP

LOVE THE SLUG

CHOP THE AVOCADO

SCOOP THE ICE CREAM

BUMP THE BUTT

GOBBLE THE TURKEY

BRUSH IT OFF

DO THE FUNGO

Emily agrees with me on all three points, but that is not why I love her. I love her because in the middle of her soul is a BALL of GOODNESS so warm and full and perfectly round that you could use it to play golf if you liked playing golf, which I don't.

A group of kids has gathered to watch our handshake. When we finish, we get a round of applause, which we ignore, because now it's time for a long, enjoyable hug.

CLAP CLAP CLAP CLAP CLAP CLAP CLAP CLAP CL
CLAP CLAP CLAP CLAP

Emily!

Moxie! I've been waiting for you!

This has been the longest three days of my life!

I need your help with something,

says Emily. I can tell
from her expression that
something serious is going
on. Which is rather exciting.

What is it? Has your cousin been
kidnapped? Are your jewels missing?

No, everyone's fine. And I don't have any
jewels. But I might have a case for you!

My eyes get big. My heart gets wide. Emily knows I've
been on the lookout for the next big case.

TELL
ME!!

5

When my dads and I got home from our camping trip, I found…

But at that moment, I see Tammy and Tracy Dublinger standing by the front door, working on their *own* secret handshake, which, if I am to be honest, they are executing with the mechanical precision of Olympic ribbon dancers.

The crowd has moved over there and is making little *ooh*ing sounds.

Tracy sees me seeing her and gives a wicked grin. Grinning wickedly is one of Tracy Dublinger's favorite pastimes.

Annabelle Adams

is constantly tormented by her nemesis, the supervillain **DR. FUNGO** who comes up with new schemes to crush happiness and inconvenience humanity as quickly as Annabelle can put a stop to them.

And I am constantly tormented by *my* nemesis, Tracy Dublinger. After Milton and I thwarted her loathsome attempt to kidnap our beloved school mascot, Eddie the great horned owl, I'd assumed she would be instantly banished to a distant moldy dungeon where all they serve is soup. But she is still among us, glaring and scheming and stealing my secret handshake.

Hey! Moxie! Over here,

says Emily, waving her hand in front of my irritated face.

So what if they have their own handshake? It will never be as great as ours.

Emily is right. Ours is the envy of seven continents, or would be if we could find a way to get it on TV.

Don't let Tracy get under your skin. She's not worth it. And, you have to admit, she's been a lot less awful lately.

7

Emily is right. Tracy has been . . . different . . . since kidnapping Eddie. Less mean. Less braggy. Less . . . Tracy. But I assume it's because she is busy at work on some even *more* dastardly scheme and is trying to keep a low profile. I don't know what it is, but I intend to find out.

Earth to Moxie!

Emily looks as if she is trying to tell me something very important.

I'm trying to tell you something very important!

Of course. The case. Does it involve a panther?

It's too crazy to describe. I need to show you.

Emily reaches into her backpack. I expect to see

a platypus skull.

Or a mangled tiara.

Or the disputed

WILL

I HEREBY LEAVE MY ESTATE TO MY PET FROG ESMERELDA.

of a Bulgarian earl.

But then the warning bell **RINGS** which means we're supposed to be at our desks sitting quietly and ready to learn in exactly five minutes.

"I have to go to the office to have my note signed for missing school on Friday," says Emily.

"But what about the case?"

"I'll tell you at first recess!"

"Aaaaarrharhr!" I like waiting as much as I like getting flu shots.

We go inside. Emily runs to the office, and I spend a moment admiring Eddie.

You're looking good, Eddie.

I say it out loud.

There, at the base of Eddie's case, is the Tiddlywhump motto,

Be wise like Eddie.

Which is what I try to do every minute of every day.

Good morning, Moxie.

I turn, and there is Principal Jones.

Tall,
intelligent,
noble, she is

THE WORLD'S
FINEST
PRINCIPAL

And, according to reliable sources, the keeper of a tank of toothless eels that's hidden below a trapdoor in her office floor. I have never met the eels and plan to keep it that way.

"Good morning, Principal Jones," I say, trying my best to look dignified and respectable and ready for anything. "And how is Tiddlywhump's finest detective?"

"Can't complain. Had two bowls of oatmeal this morning. Feeling fortified."

I do not know why I am telling Principal Jones about my breakfast. To be entirely honest, she makes me a little nervous.

"I'm glad to hear it."

"Yes. Yes. Nutrition is my middle name."

I hope that Principal Jones realizes that this is just a phrase that means nutrition is important to me. My real middle name is Minerva.

We stand there for a minute, smiling together at history's most lovable owl.

"It sure is good to have Eddie back where he belongs," she says before giving me a dignified nod and heading back to her office.

It sure is, I think. I give Eddie one last loving glance and head down the hall to the fourth-grade classroom, bracing myself for another Monday at the mercy of Mrs. Bunyan, history's *least* lovable fourth-grade teacher.

I slide into my seat and am wondering what lies in store for me, when I suddenly notice that Mrs. Bunyan is now a cheerful bald man with bright orange glasses and an oversized smile.

11

CHAPTER 2: TWO BIG PROBLEMS

Good morning, class, says the smiling man.

My name is Mr. Shine. If you haven't heard already, Mrs. Bunyan decided to retire. I am the new fourth-grade teacher. It is my genuine pleasure to meet you.

This is the greatest news I've heard in a long time! Mrs. Bunyan and I were about as different as the opposite ends of a magnet.

Mr. Shine seems like a pleasant sort of person. He smiles with every word as if he just adopted a kitten and really wants you to pet it.

While we sit there getting used to this exciting new information, Mr. Shine explains the rules of his classroom, including his policy regarding Owl Points.

At Tiddlywhump, you start each term with 100 Owl Points and lose one whenever you do something wrong. Mrs. Bunyan loved nothing more than taking away Owl Points. One time, I lost one for sneezing three times in less than a minute.

AHCHOOO!

AHHCHOOO!

LOSE A POINT!

Mr. Shine tells us that he doesn't believe in punishment and instead plans to reward us for good behavior.

"Reward us with what?" says Tracy Dublinger.

Tracy is the queen of good behavior. She never met a rule she didn't want to follow.

"With *smiles*," says Mr. Shine.

"What's that?" says Tracy. "Some sort of stamp?"

Some teachers give out Owl Stamps when you raise your hand nicely or spell a really complicated word correctly,

ONE OWL STAMP!

googolplex

ONE OWL STAMP!

and if we collect enough of them, the entire class gets some sort of prize, such as five extra minutes of recess or the chance to watch a video about elephants.

Mr. Shine is blinking as if he doesn't understand what Tracy means.

No, I mean, an *actual* smile.

This smile,

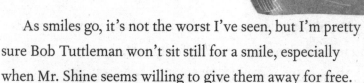

he says, pointing to his mouth and giving us a sample of the smile in question.

As smiles go, it's not the worst I've seen, but I'm pretty sure Bob Tuttleman won't sit still for a smile, especially when Mr. Shine seems willing to give them away for free.

"Now I'd like to get to know each of *you.* Tell me about yourself," he says, looking right at Holly.

"Me?" says Holly.

"Yes," says Mr. Shine, smiling. "What should I know about you?"

"Hmm . . . ," says Holly. "I have two cats."

"I love cats!" says Mr. Shine. "What are their names?"

"Bortles and Tuppence."

"My cat is named Gremlin," says Mr. Shine.

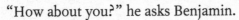

"How about you?" he asks Benjamin.

"I have an iguana named Evelyn."

"How *interesting*!"

I am suspicious. In my experience,
fourth-grade teachers are only *interested* in useless facts
and impossible spelling tests and scowling when you make
mistakes. They do not smile. They do not ask about
your iguana.

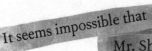

It seems impossible that Mr. Shine is an actual teacher,

BWAH HA HA HA HAAA!!

and I wonder if he might, instead, be an undercover henchman

or a renegade spy.

Or possibly . . . something worse that I can't even imagine
this early in the day.

My detective mind is doing backflips. As Annabelle
Adams often says, "the most complicated explanation is
occasionally the right one."

Mr. Shine reminds me of Elwood Theopolous, a seemingly pleasant pastry chef who throws Annabelle a cupcake party (Volume 29: *Fake and Bake*) every day for a month until she eventually lets down her guard.

When Annabelle sets down her briefcase of top secret medical research so she can hold two cupcakes at once, Elwood tosses the briefcase into a volcanic fissure, denying the residents of Lower Thrombonia a cure to the chronic hiccuping that has plagued the town for generations.

HIC!
HIC!
HIC!
HIC!
HIC!
HIC!
HIC!

Of course, a few chapters later, Annabelle develops a cure of her own, using nothing but a day-old bagel and a tube of ANTIFUNGAL FOOT CREAM.

What makes you happiest, Bob?

My grandma.

What about her?

She tells stories about when she was a little girl.

Such as?

She didn't even have a TV.

There are several loud GASPS.

Anything else?

She didn't even have a cell phone.

More gasps. It's clear that no one believes him.

Thank you, Bob.

As weird as it is that Mr. Shine is still asking us questions, it's even more surprising that Bob Tuttleman is sitting still and answering them. I've known Bob since kindergarten, and this might be the first time he's actually paid attention to anything a teacher has said.

This goes on for more than an hour. Mr. Shine asks questions and listens and smiles and smiles and smiles. I learn things I'd never known.

Freddie is afraid of butterflies.
Grace speaks Danish.

Jeg har
elleve katte!

Jose has an extensive collection of license plates.

The other kids are having the time of their lives. I seem to be the only one who realizes Mr. Shine is probably collecting information to use against us later.

Mr. Shine finishes chatting with Sandy about her family trip to a big museum in Arkansas and turns his eyes to me.

How about you, Moxie?

Mr. Shine smiles as if he's trying to win a contest with the sun. He *almost* seems like an entirely kind and trustworthy person—which is why I'm pretty sure he isn't.

UH, You WIN.

I fold my arms and look skeptical.

"What *about* me?"

"Tell us something about yourself."

"Nothing much to tell." One of Annabelle's most important rules of thumb is never revealing unnecessary personal details.

"What's your favorite color?"

BLOOD RED. The question seems harmless enough.

"How interesting! And your favorite hobby?"

EXPOSING INJUSTICE! It's important that Mr. Shine knows who he is dealing with.

"My *goodness*. What's your—?"

"Excuse me, please, but I have a few questions for *you*," I say, doing my best to look fierce.

But Mr. Shine's smile just gets bigger.

"How wonderful! Go ahead."

"What's *your* favorite color?"

"Blue."

Ugh. So predictable.

"What's *your* favorite hobby?"

"Making people smile."

Ugh! Mr. Shine is worse than boring the boring main character in the boring chapter book series Milton is obsessed with. I need to get to the bottom of whatever he's up to. So I try a different approach.

Danny Doogood,

What did you do this past weekend?

I ask, leaning forward in my seat and lowering my eyebrows as Annabelle might, hoping Mr. Shine will break down and reveal his true intentions.

Instead, he gives an even bigger smile and says,

I got a job.

I want to ask what sort of dastardly things he had to do to get that job, but before I can get the words out, he says,

And what did *you* do?

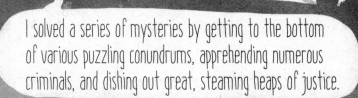

I solved a series of mysteries by getting to the bottom of various puzzling conundrums, apprehending numerous criminals, and dishing out great, steaming heaps of justice.

I may be exaggerating a little, but it's definitely how I *wish* I'd spent the weekend.

Mr. Shine's eyes get wider, but at no point does he stop smiling. It's clear he knows he's met his match. We are locked in a staring/smiling contest when the bell rings, letting us know it's time for first recess, which is incredible because school started *two whole hours ago*, and Mr. Shine hasn't taught us *one single thing*.

"Thank you, Moxie. I feel like I know you better now," says Mr. Shine, giving me a look that means

To Be
CONTINUED

I want to talk to Emily about whatever is inside her backpack. But because she is so good and generous and kind, Emily volunteers as one of

PRINCIPAL JONES'S
RECESS HELPERS

which means she spends the first ten minutes of first recess doing good deeds, like helping kindergartners blow their noses or organizing rubber bands in the art room. Emily asked me if I wanted to join, but I had to refuse. Because my clients need me.

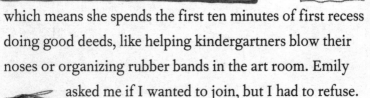

Plus, to be entirely truthful, I really *like* recess.

I grab my coat and head out to the bench where Milton and I sit to consider new cases.

Milton is already on the bench. I look around. For what seems like the millionth day in a row, no one is waiting to talk to us.

Good day, Milton.

Good day, Moxie.

Milton is reading a book about Danny Doogood—a goody two-shoes of a second grader who is as boring as a  STICK OF BUTTER

and spends all day, every day, following every rule and telling everybody else what to do.

Danny lives in a boring house in a boring neighborhood. He even has a boring dog.

Danny does not fight crime. He does not solve mysteries. Danny's reason for living is being on time. And doing his chores without being asked. And picking up trash from other people's yards. Danny apologizes when he sneezes too loud. Instead of an apple, he gives his teachers apple pies.

"Ugh," I say. Danny makes my eyeballs itch.

"As Danny Doogood often says,

'If you're upset about something, you should use actual words,'"

 says Milton without looking up from his book.

I glare at Milton and use some actual words that Danny would definitely not approve of.

Milton says nothing. There's nothing to say. We sit and we wait and we wait. I look around at all the kids who are *not* coming to talk to us.

 Why don't we have any cases? I ask.

Where is the calamity?!

Milton looks up from his book.

 I'm glad you asked. I think that—

My guess is that the criminals are afraid because they know they don't stand a chance.

Or …

perhaps it's that we—

Maybe it has something to do with the moon.

I look up. The moon is not available for viewing.

 I've been thinking we should—

Hello, I say.

Someone is standing there.

24

It's a boy from Milton's class. His name is John. He is about as interesting as a paper clip. Nevertheless, he is a potential client, and so I give him a serious look and wave my hand majestically. "Hello, John. Welcome to our bench. What seems to be the problem?"

"Don't hurt me!" says John.

"I'm not going to hurt you, John. I'm here to *help* you."

"Whew."

> I assume you've come to us with a serious problem. Something requiring the assistance of a highly trained problem-solving mastermind and her trusty sidekick?

Milton shoots me a glare. He does not like being called a *sidekick*, but he's even less fond of *lackey*, which is the only other word I can think of for what he is.

> What Moxie means is, can we help you with anything?

I'm . . . I'm looking for my ball, says John.

It bounced over there somewhere.

We look around. Milton finds John's ball in a clump of tall grass.

"Thanks," says John.

"Don't mention it," says Milton as John takes his ball and wanders away.

"Really, *please* don't mention it," I say. I can't have it getting out that we've been reduced to helping first graders find lost balls.

But Mom is always encouraging me to put a positive spin on things, and so I do. "There you have it, Milton. Business is really picking up."

"About that . . . ," says Milton. "Maybe we'd get more clients if we did a little . . . advertising."

"What do you mean?"

"To let people know we're here and

OPEN for Business."

"People *know*! Of course they know." I am outraged at the suggestion that people do not know.

"We pretty much just look like two kids sitting on a bench."

What are you suggesting? A *TV commercial*?

I like this idea. Emily and I could do our secret handshake.

Maybe a sign?

And maybe some buttons.

I do like signs. And I'm a big fan of buttons. But making them is too much trouble.

And COMPLETELY UNNECESSARY

I pat Milton on the head and look into his eyes. "It's widely known that I am the greatest detective in the history of fourth grade. We will sit on this bench until the world comes calling."

Milton says nothing. There's nothing to say. Because he knows I'm right.

A few more painful minutes pass. I'm almost to the point of *causing* a problem for us to solve when Emily comes bounding over and sticks out her elbow. We do our secret handshake, and I'm impressed with us all over again.

"Hi, Emily," says Milton.

"Hi, Milton!" says Emily. "I'm glad you're both here," she says, reaching into her backpack.

I'm convinced it contains a three-headed python or a pouch of pirate's gold.

Instead, Emily pulls out an envelope. Inside, there is a piece of paper that says:

Emily——
I want you to know how much I appreciate you. You are good. You are kind. You are generous. You make this world a better place. I consider myself fortunate to know you. I hope you will always be true to yourself.
—The person you'd least expect

It's a perfect description of Emily. She really is the best.

Who's it from?

That's the thing! There's no signature! All it says is, "The person you'd least expect."

And who's that?

I have no idea!

How did you get it?

It was waiting in the mailbox when my dads and I got home from our trip. And there's no return address!

So you have no clue who sent it?

None at all! But I *have* to find out so I can thank whoever it is. Can you guys help?

Milton and I look at each other. I can tell he's as excited as I am. *This* is the case we've been waiting for. There is *mystery*! And *intrigue*! And the distinct possibility of *saving the world*!

This one is the REAL McCOY!

I am full of questions for Emily, but recess is about to end. "All right," I say. "Let's talk at lunch to come up with a plan."

As Emily and I line up with the other fourth graders, I notice something suspicious. Mr. Shine is chatting with Bob Tuttleman. That is not the suspicious thing. Bob is always good for a little chitchat. The suspicious thing is that Mr. Shine is wearing a bright pink hand-knit hat with a lopsided purple daisy on the side.

I know this hat. It belongs to someone I know. Or *used* to know. Someone I don't much like but am now ever so slightly worried about.

THE HAT BELONGS TO MRS. BUNYAN

She wore it every time it was cold outside and sometimes even when it wasn't. She was wearing it the last time I saw her.

Suddenly, I wonder if, in spite of his smiling-nice-guy routine, Mr. Shine might have something to do with Mrs. Bunyan's disappearance. Teachers don't *usually* retire in the middle of the school year. And Mrs. Bunyan seemed to like her job *so much*. I've never seen someone get so much pleasure out of yelling at kids.

What if Mrs. Bunyan didn't just *decide* to retire? What if Mr. Shine *kidnapped* her and stole her job and took her hat? What if he's holding her prisoner in a rickety fishing boat off the coast of Newfoundland?

Don't get me wrong—Mrs. Bunyan and I were never the best of friends. But I can't stand the thought of anyone being treated unfairly.

I'm onto you,

I say in a menacing whisper as Mr. Shine stands there smiling in his fuzzy pink hat. I say it loud enough to hear myself, and I like how it sounds.

CHAPTER 3: THE SQUIGGLER

The day moves slower than the week leading up to my birthday. All I want to do is work on Emily's case. But instead I'm stuck listening to a person who refuses to behave like a teacher and might be a deranged kidnapper.

My classmates do the same irritating, distracting, rule-breaking fourth-grade things they always do, but no one gets a death stare. No one loses an Owl Point. With Mrs. Bunyan, you always knew where you stood:

right in the middle of her own private dartboard.

But no matter what we do, Mr. Shine just keeps on smiling.

While he interrogates Donna about her love of mermaids, I think about Emily's letter. One thing doesn't add up: In my experience, people don't usually do nice things just for the sake of it. Sometimes, things that *seem* well intentioned end up being exactly the opposite.

In Annabelle Adams, Girl Detective,
Volume 6:

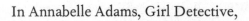

Death by Envelope,

everyone in the peaceful
town of

Historic
BLEVIN

gets an anonymous
invitation to a
croquet-themed summer
picnic to be held in the
scenic countryside.

I'M EXTREMELY
NICE! AND
TRUSTWORTHY!

Since the envelopes all have
teddy bear stamps, everyone assumes
the person who sent them must be
extremely nice and trustworthy.

But, of course, the person who sent
them is Dr. Fungo, who is the opposite
of nice and allergic to trust.

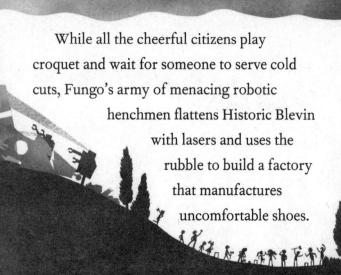

While all the cheerful citizens play croquet and wait for someone to serve cold cuts, Fungo's army of menacing robotic henchmen flattens Historic Blevin with lasers and uses the rubble to build a factory that manufactures uncomfortable shoes.

The similarities between Annabelle's story and Emily's situation are impossible to ignore. Which means someone is trying to trick Emily into *thinking* they are nice and good and well meaning. Which means I need to figure out who it is before my best friend gets historically

FLATTENED.

The lunch bell rings. Emily, Milton, and I get our trays and find an empty table.

"Here's the situation," I say. "We have no clues. No broken glass. No bloody fingerprints. No blind witness who can describe the sound of the criminal's jagged breathing."

"Jagged breathing?" asks Milton.

"It's possible he had a respiratory ailment."

"He?"

"There's a 50% chance the criminal was a he."

Milton looks at me with exasperation.

"Criminal?"

"Everyone knows it's unethical—and maybe *illegal*—to leave important documents unsigned!"

Emily looks distraught. "I don't want him—or her—to get in trouble! This is the nicest thing anyone has ever done for me."

"I admit it *seems* nice. But it could be the first step in a dastardly plan to . . ."

I can't decide whether or not to tell Emily how much danger she's in. For the time being, I downplay the peril.

". . . replace the mayor with a less effective mayor."

Emily gasps.

"The point is, *we know nothing*!"

"We know a *few* things," says Milton.

"Like what?" asks Emily, her big eyes full of hope.

Usually, letters have stamps on them.

Milton is right. There is no stamp, which means that . . .

Whoever wrote this letter put it in your mailbox.

Which means, whoever it is *probably* doesn't live in Argentina, I add.

"You guys are *good*," says Emily.

"How long were you out of town?" asks Milton.

"Three days."

"So there's no way of knowing when during that time the letter was delivered."

Milton is right. This case keeps getting tougher.

Criminals often return to the scene of the crime, I say.

I know this because Annabelle has, on six separate occasions, caught crooks who were cackling wickedly at a crime scene instead of hiding out in run-down motels on the outskirts of town.

But has there been a *crime?* asks Emily.

For now, let's call it an *incident,* I say.

Or maybe some nice person sent Emily a nice note, says Milton, shooting me an irritated look.

Emily looks *RELIEVED,* which is the

WORST POSSIBLE OUTCOME.

What Milton is suggesting is *technically* possible, but much more likely, this is the first step in a string of diabolical deeds designed to ensure Emily's

TRAGIC • DOWNFALL,

I say, deciding the only way to keep my best friend safe is to tell the absolute truth.

Emily looks extremely worried.

Milton places his hand gently on her shoulder. "As Danny Doogood often observes, 'The simplest explanation is usually the correct one.'"

"That makes sense," says Emily, looking at Milton as if he's said something really wise.

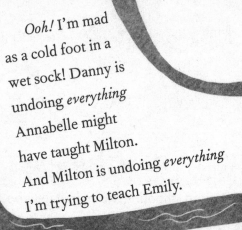

Ooh! I'm mad as a cold foot in a wet sock! Danny is undoing *everything* Annabelle might have taught Milton. And Milton is undoing *everything* I'm trying to teach Emily.

"There's another clue," I say, pointing to the envelope.

"What?" asks Emily.

"Look at this purple squiggle. On one hand, it could be nothing."

"But on the other hand, it could be *something*," says Milton.

"Exactly." Finally, Milton has said something useful.

Now that we have a few clues, I'm hoping he'll use his great big brain to tie them all together.

I LOOK AT HIM.

HE LOOKS AT ME.

The great big brain seems to have nothing.

"The only connection we have to the squiggler is the mailbox," says Milton.

> I am excited! Suddenly, our nemesis has a name.

THE SQUIGGLER

And Milton is right, the Squiggler must have put the mysterious letter in Emily's mailbox.

"But how do we figure out who the Squiggler *is*?" asks Emily.

That is the question I'm chewing on as lunch ends and Emily and I walk back to class and Mr. Shine continues to investigate our insides with his endless questions.

"Who's next?" asks Mr. Shine, looking around the room before resting his eyes on Megan.

"What's something about you that no one else knows, Megan?"

"One time I swallowed four quarters."

"*Oh?* Why?"

"I wanted to see what would happen."

"And what happened?"

"Nothing at first."

"And then?"

"They eventually came back out."

"How *interesting*."

Finally, the day ends, and I meet Milton in front of the school. As we walk home, I want to talk about our case, but Milton has other ideas.

To continue our conversation from earlier . . .

About the Squiggler?

No, about our lack of business.

I am tempted to point out that we have just landed a new, fantastic case, but Milton is not done.

"Maybe we need to make ourselves seem like an *official* detective agency."

I like the sound of that. "Go on."

"I was thinking that maybe we should be . . . partners."

The word makes me SHUDDER.

Partners are equal. Partners are approximately the same height. Partners wear identical hats.

Milton is at best a sidekick and at worst a lackey. Milton comes up to my elbow. Milton is positively gnomish.

I do the hard work, collecting clues, intimidating suspects, and gathering essential evidence. Milton does the easy stuff, analyzing the data, connecting the dots, and reaching the conclusions. Don't get me wrong. He can be useful. But is he a *partner*? He is not.

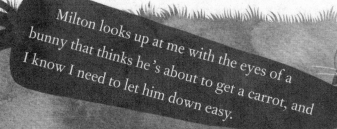

Milton looks up at me with the eyes of a bunny that thinks he's about to get a carrot, and I know I need to let him down easy.

"Maybe someday," I say. "No need to rush things. First you need to complete your training."

Milton scowls, and I don't blame him. It's no fun to be a sidekick, but he has to pay his dues.

When she was in training, Annabelle had to lick and seal 500 envelopes without taking a single sip of water and then had to stand completely still—

without even saying ouch–

while a cheerful grandmother pinched her cheek 900 times, to prove everlasting dedication to her mentor and sensei, a ninja named Ninja.

Apparently, Milton is not done. "If people knew that I was a full *partner* . . . that there were *two* detectives . . . I think it might help business."

But since he doesn't seem to be getting the point, I talk a little louder. "This agency needs only one detective. And make no mistake, the sidekick is *optional*!"

8-TRACK
(useless)

DOT MATRIX
(obsolete)

CHAI TEA
(redundant)

THE APPENDIX
(unnecessary)

You know I don't like being called *sidekick*.

Would you prefer *lackey*?

I know that Milton does not prefer *lackey*.

No, I would not.

I am about to ask Milton how he would feel about *gnomish* when a girl named Shelby rushes up to us on the sidewalk looking like she is being chased by a herd of extremely hungry jackals.

HELP! HELP!! I NEED YOUR HELP!

CHAPTER 4: PROVING HIMSELF

"What seems to be the—"

"My unicorn ring! I had it, then I lost it. And I *need* to get it back!"

"Do not despair, Shelby. I'm sure we can help you if you'll just calm—"

"I will never be happy again!" Shelby is ramping up for a good cry.

"Where did you see it last?" Milton asks.

"I know *exactly* where it is," says Shelby.

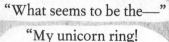

Down there!

She points to the sewer grate, her lower lip wiggling with sadness.

Hmmm . . . .

I say, wondering if my love of adventure might just have met its limit.

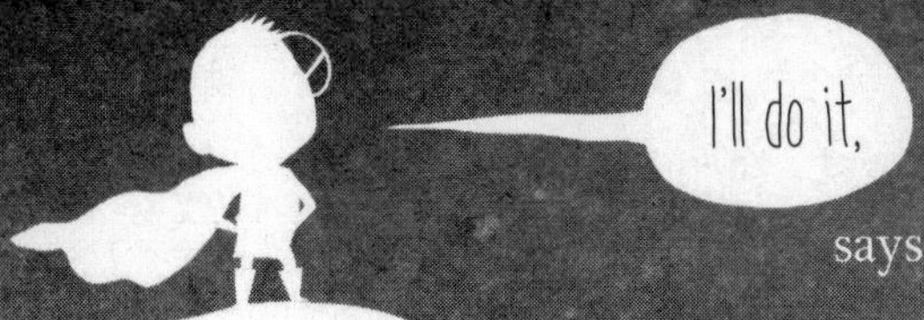

I'll do it,

says Milton.

"You will?" says Shelby.

"You *will*?" I say.

"Yes," says Milton, puffing out
his chest. "To prove my dedication.
To show you what I'm made of." Milton
gives me a long look. "But if I find it, will you
consider making me a partner?"

"Sure," I say. And I mean it. I will *consider* just
about anything.

A few minutes later, I am holding
on to one end of a rope while Milton
dangles from the other. He is making
my job difficult by thrashing around.

Hurry up!

I suggest.

I don't see it!

45

Keep looking,

I say with one side of my mouth

while smiling confidently at Shelby with the other.

Shelby, before we can go any further, I need to collect payment.

"But you haven't found my ring yet."

"I'm sorry. But I need to be sure you'll be able to pay for our services. That will be one dollar."

"*A whole dollar?*" Shelby looks as if I've demanded one of her kidneys.

"Yes," I say. It's the standard rate. Technically, I could charge her more since the operation requires going into a sewer, but I'm giving her a break since it's Milton down there and not me. Avoiding sewers is one of the best things about having a sidekick.

Shelby digs around in her pockets. "Here," she says, handing me a dollar as if she were saying good-bye to her very best friend.

"Thank you," I say, shoving it into the deepest part of my pocket.

I try to never talk about money in front of Milton. As a sidekick, he is not entitled to actual payment. I have told him before that all the experience he's getting is worth tens if not twenties of dollars, but he keeps insisting the arrangement isn't fair.

Milton lurches. My feet slip.

But the case is not yet solved. Milton is new to the detective business, and he still hasn't learned how it works. Shelby paid her dollar. We promised to find her ring. And so we will. It's what we do. It's who we *are*.

I'm about to tell Shelby how lucky she is to know us when I notice a great big expression on her face.

"Oh!" she says, sheepishly pulling something shiny from her pocket. "I guess I didn't drop it after all."

Whenever a problem is solved and a case is closed,

A SHIVER OF PURE DELIGHT

shoots straight from my heart to the tips of my fingers and toes. Today, the delight is so enormous that I accidentally loosen my grip on the rope *just a little*.

What happens next is a SPLASH

followed by the sound of someone taking great gulping breaths followed by a cry of undignified outrage.

MOXIEEEEEEEEE !!!! PULL. ME. UP. NOW!!

I am reluctant. Not because there's any good reason for Milton to stay down there, but because I'm a little afraid of what he is going to do or say when he comes back up. And so I pretend I can't hear him. I am, after all, still assisting our client.

What about my DOLLAR? asks Shelby. She's holding out her hand as if there is a chance I'll put something in it.

People's problems always seem so much less important after they've been solved. Which is why I always make them pay up front.

"I'm sorry, Shelby, but your dollar has already been spent." Shelby looks confused. Which is exactly the point. Before she can object, I tell her that, at this very moment, a team of Swiss physicists is using her dollar to create a new kind of laser capable of teleporting guacamole to places where avocados don't grow.

Shelby blinks a few times, realizes she's been defeated, and wanders away. Which means I have no more excuses not to pull Milton back up. When he emerges from the sewer, he looks like a soggy sandwich that has just been thrown up by a seasick whale.

He's stinky and grimy, and his teeth are chattering so badly I can't understand what he's saying.

I lead my smelly ice cube of a brother inside, draw him a bubble bath, and, because I'm feeling generous, read aloud to him from Annabelle Adams, Volume 51:

The Not-So-Silver Lining.

It's the one where Annabelle is appointed grand duke of a tiny island nation in the Arctic Ocean. Annabelle accepts her new position without realizing that the grand duke's responsibilities include knitting holiday sweaters for the nation's 23 citizens and 679 penguins.

Dad comes home and checks on us. Milton says nothing about his accidental swimming lesson, which makes me rather proud of him. Even though Dad is the **WORLD'S GREATEST FATHER**

knowing the details of our cases could put him in utmost danger. Milton refuses to come down to the table for dinner. Dad and I eat leftover lasagna and stale corn chips wrapped in steamed tortillas and chat about our days.

How are your cases?

We have a new one. It's a doozy.

Does the fate of the world hang in the balance?

Do you even have to ask?

Dad smiles. "How's Milton?"

"Fine. He's just fine."

"He seems upset. Any idea why?"

"You know, he's . . . Milton."

"He certainly is." Dad gives me a look that lets me know he knows there's something I'm not saying, so I fake a big yawn and take my plate to the sink. "I'd better get to bed. Big day tomorrow. Saving the world takes so much energy."

"The world is lucky that you're here," says Dad. He gives me a **HUG.** And then he gives me another one. The second hug is from Mom. He always makes the Mom hug twice as big.

On the way to my bedroom, I check in on Milton, who is still in the bath.

Feeling better? I ask through the door.

I'm fine, he says.

Well?

Well what?

Are you convinced? he says.

Of what?

That I am ready to be a partner!

I am convinced . . . that you will be. Someday.

But I went into the sewer! I proved myself!

You did . . . but . . . you didn't find the ring.

BECAUSE IT WASN'T THERE!

That's beside the point.

Go away,

says Milton.

I hope you can see that—

GO AWAY!

he says,
much louder this time.

And so I leave him there, stewing in his thoughts, and get into bed.

As I close my eyes, I wonder if I'll wake up in the morning to a grumpy sidekick or a 40-pound raisin.

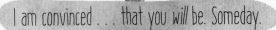

THAT'S 40.25
POUNDS, THANK
YOU VERY MUCH!

CHAPTER 5: UNITED WE STAND

The alarm goes off. I do my morning exercises (a detective must be fit). I do my morning reading (a detective must be sound of mind). I practice my single eyebrow lift (a detective must be able to effortlessly enchant an unsuspecting archduke at a costume ball).

When I come downstairs for breakfast, Milton is using a tiny screwdriver to attach a tiny wire to a tiny motor, which is attached to the side of a

SHINY METAL CUBE.

Usually when Milton is really mad, he leaves the moment I come into the room, but today he sits calmly, not looking at me but not quite ignoring me, either.

"Good morning," I say, as if I hadn't dropped him in a river of cold sewage the day before.

Milton sort of grunts, which is as much as I could expect on a good day. He's so focused on whatever he's making that I can't help but look.

There are levers and switches and lightbulbs and wires. There's a keypad and a tiny screen and what looks like a speaker.

Milton's birthday was three weeks ago, and all he asked for was "parts." On the morning of his birthday, there was just one huge box waiting in the middle of the living room. It clanked and crunched and brought a smile the size of the moon to Milton's face. He opened it and shrieked with delight. As a general rule, Milton does not shriek. He rarely even smiles. But somehow, a box of stuff that looks like robot poop made him giddy as a cartoon monkey.

That's all he got. That and all three awful Danny Doogood books.

IT'S SHAPING UP TO BE A DOOGOOD DAY!

Milton attaches a tennis ball to an orange wire that leads into the mysterious machine.

"What is it?" I can't help myself.

"A lie detector," he says without looking up.

Of course I know *all about* lie detectors. Annabelle Adams has one installed in her wristwatch, and all she has to do is get within **40 FEET OF A SUSPECT** to figure out whether or not they are telling the truth. I have always wanted a lie detector. It would make solving cases **SO MUCH EASIER.**

"How does it work?" I ask, pretending I'm only mildly interested.

"First put this on your head." Milton hands me a baseball cap with various wires and lightbulbs attached.

"Then hold this in your left hand." He hands me the tennis ball. I feel half ridiculous and half thrilled.

"Next tell me the truth."

I'm hungry.

The machine makes a squeak and a little green lightbulb comes on.

"*Truth*," says Milton. "Now tell me a lie."

I love chicken noodle soup.

The machine makes a sound like

A FLOCK OF ANGRY SEAGULLS

attacking an unsuspecting mailman, and three red lights blink on and off.

"*Lie*. Now I'll ask you an actual question. Have you read Danny Doogood, Book 2: *Doing Gooder*?"

Milton begged me to read Danny Doogood, Book 1:
Doing Good, and so I did, even though it was
worse than eating a spoonful of

Then he begged me to read Book 2. Let me be clear:
I have not and will not read another page about Danny and
his dopey, dumb life. But since Milton *asked* me to read the
second book and I *said I would* . . . I say . . .

"Yes."

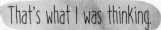
The angry seagulls return.

"*Lie.*"

"You're right," I admit.

Milton looks extremely pleased. And I'm extremely
impressed. As I pour my cereal, a delicious thought occurs
to me.

The lie detector! We can use
it to identify the Squiggler!

That's what I was thinking.

I have to admit, Milton is a lot more useful sidekick than
I sometimes give him credit for.

I am about to ask if he can also build me a jetpack and a time machine when I notice an envelope sitting on my place mat. An envelope that wasn't there a moment ago.

All it says is:

ATTN:
Moxie McCoy

I open the envelope and pull out a beautiful document.

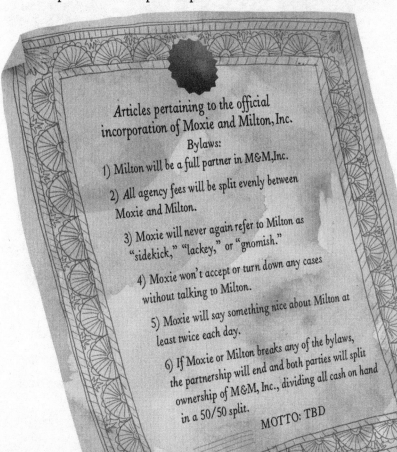

Articles pertaining to the official incorporation of Moxie and Milton, Inc.

Bylaws:

1) Milton will be a full partner in M&M, Inc.

2) All agency fees will be split evenly between Moxie and Milton.

3) Moxie will never again refer to Milton as "sidekick," "lackey," or "gnomish."

4) Moxie won't accept or turn down any cases without talking to Milton.

5) Moxie will say something nice about Milton at least twice each day.

6) If Moxie or Milton breaks any of the bylaws, the partnership will end and both parties will split ownership of M&M, Inc., dividing all cash on hand in a 50/50 split.

MOTTO: TBD

"What's this all about?" I ask.

"It's time," says Milton.

"For what?"

"For me to be a full *partner*."

I do not like this. I do not like this at all. This document is the opposite of everything I stand for!

But I do really like how it looks. *The official-looking border! The shiny gold seal!*

But the *words*! They are outrageous! *Full partner?!* This is rubbish!

"Rubbish" is what Annabelle Adams says when she needs to let people know she's outraged while working undercover as a feisty British housekeeper.

I'm tempted to burn the document in the fireplace before flushing the ashes down six toilets on three continents, but I can't help but notice again how amazing it looks. And how official it sounds, especially the words *pertaining* and *incorporation*.

Milton is sitting there, gazing at me like a puppy that wants to know whether or not you're going to finish your sandwich.

"What about this?" I ask, pointing to the bit about the motto and trying to sound skeptical.

"We need a motto."

I am tempted to disagree, but I can't. Annabelle Adams has a fantastic motto:

"Trust no one but yourself."

But Annabelle's motto wouldn't *quite* work for Milton and me since there are two of us. "What do *you* think our motto should be?"

"'United we stand,'" he says without hesitation, as if he's been thinking about it for a long time.

"Not bad," I say. I am also considering

"To the death"

AND

"With the furious vengeance of a billion suns,"

but neither feels quite right.

"Our motto should tell people what we stand for," says Milton.

"And what do we stand for?"

JUSTICE! I think about that. Nothing makes me madder than when people are treated unfairly, even Mrs. Bunyan. Justice is a no-brainer.

AND UNITY! Unity? Unity is okay as long as Milton doesn't mean EQUAL unity. I will always be in charge because I am older and wiser and braver and so much taller. Milton seems to be asking for something more than unity.

He reaches under the table
and pulls out a button.

I LOVE THE BUTTON. IT IS SO BEAUTIFUL WITH ITS BLUE BACKGROUND AND GREEN LETTERS. AND I LIKE HOW THE WORDS RHYME. I WANT TO PIN IT TO MY SHIRT AT THIS VERY MOMENT.

Against all better judgment, I find myself agreeing that it is an excellent motto.

Can I have that button right now? I ask.

Of course,

says Milton, pinning it to my shirt
before pulling out another and
pinning it to his shirt. We're sitting
there with matching buttons.

It all feels so OFFICIAL. As if it was meant to be.

Milton pulls out a pen.

Sign here

I am feeling hot and rushed. I look at the paper again. There's so much I don't like. The 50/50 split. Milton's sudden promotion from sidekick to full partner. *Partner.* I don't like how it sounds. I don't like what it *means*.

Here you go,

says Milton, pushing the pen across the table, his voice as comforting as a bunny in a bonnet.

I hardly know what my hand is doing as I pick up the pen. It's like someone else is moving my fingers. A gentle voice inside my head is saying, *Don't worry. Everything is going to be just fine.*

Before I know it, the paper is signed and Milton is sliding it into his pocket.

I feel like I've made a terrible mistake.

"Let me have that back," I say.

Just then, Milton reaches under the table again and pulls out an enormous sign.

MOXIE & milton, INC.

UNITED WE STAND ★ ★ ★ JUSTICE WE DEMAND

I let out a gasp.
The good kind.

Pretty great, right?

THE SIGN IS MAGNIFICENT.

I decide to give this thing a try. Maybe Milton will be an acceptable partner. He certainly knows how to make excellent signs. And buttons. And lie detectors.

Dad comes in and grabs some toast.

Good morning, he says.

Good morning, we say.

What's this? he asks, looking at the sign and giving Milton a wink.

Clearly, Dad was part of this operation.

I am tempted to be hurt, but instead, I look down at my button and try to have a positive attitude. Mom is always talking about THE POWER OF A ⚡ POSITIVE ⚡ ATTITUDE ⚡ and she is the most intelligent person I've ever met in my entire life.

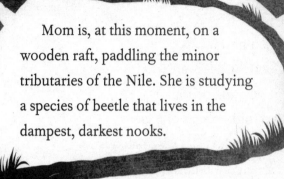

Mom is, at this moment, on a wooden raft, paddling the minor tributaries of the Nile. She is studying a species of beetle that lives in the dampest, darkest nooks.

The beetle is behaving strangely, and so Mom, being the world's most amazing entomologist, has been called in to get to the bottom of things.

I wish that she were here to see what a positive attitude I'm having, but she is doing important work that will almost certainly change the course of history.

Which is why I always try so hard to do important work, too.

CHAPTER 6: OPEN FOR BUSINESS

When I get to Mr. Shine's classroom, a nightmare is unfolding. All the desks are in different places, and on top of each one is a folded piece of paper letting us know who each desk belongs to. This is strange and upsetting and unacceptable. But as I search for my desk, I realize the awfulness is just beginning.

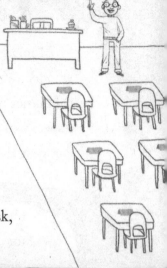

I find my name. I find my desk. It's stranded between horrible and even worse. Between full moon and werewolf. Between Tammy and Tracy Dublinger.

I stay standing as long as I can, but finally I can delay no longer and slide into my seat. It's like being the meat in a

MOLDY SANDWICH.

I feel Tracy breathing on my arm.

 MORNING!" says Mr. Shine, as cheerful as a clown in a commercial. "I thought it would be fun to mix things up a bit. I find that when you sit in one place for too long, you start thinking in one way for too long."

He has a good point. Annabelle Adams does her best thinking while eating ice cream.

And when she's feeling stuck on a case, she will often travel to another country and eat ice cream there.

But I am stuck in a desolate wasteland between two hostile nations with no ice cream parlors in sight.

"All right," says Mr. Shine. "I've tried very hard to remember all your names, and I think I've finally got it." He puts his class list down and looks at Chaz intently.

 And you are . . . *Elliot,* says Mr. Shine with a confident smile.

 Nope, says Chaz, who looks *so much like a Chaz* that the mistake seems unforgivable.

 Oh, shucks! Of course. You're . . . *Chaz,* he says, looking at Chaz,

 and *you're* Sandy, he says, looking at Freddie.

 Nope! says Freddie, laughing.

I'm Sandy, says Sandy, laughing, too.

 And I'm not doing well *at all,* says Mr. Shine.

I must have smog in my noggin.

HA HA HA HA HA HA HA HA HA H'A HA HA

Now the other kids laugh, and I start to laugh with them. But then I stop in my tracks and reach into my memory bank.

I have only heard *one other human being on planet Earth* use the phrase *smog in my noggin.*

One day, when I might not have been paying 100% attention to Mrs. Bunyan's lecture on the water cycle, she interrupted my deep, important thoughts by asking me the official name for rain, and I couldn't for the life of me think of

PRECIPITATION

and so she suggested in front of the entire class that I probably had *smog in my noggin.*

Which means . . . not only has Mr. Shine stolen Mrs. Bunyan's hat, but *now he is also using her extremely unusual phrase*!

My mind is reeling as the recess bell rings. I'm barely
out the door to the playground when I see Milton sprinting
toward me.

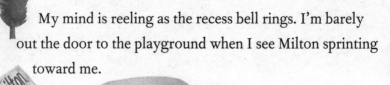

Are you ready?

he says, panting and smiling
and panting some more.

Ready for what?

To officially open the agency!

I am ready to focus on finding the Squiggler, but Milton
holds up the sign, and I realize what a terrible mistake I've
made. Beyond the beautiful letters and magnificent colors,
there is one enormous problem—one I *should* have seen this
morning, but somehow missed in the pleasant golden seal
haze. There are *two* McCoys on
this sign, side by side,

exactly the same size.

I head toward our bench, but Milton is walking in the other direction.

"Where are you going?"

"To that bench over there. You know what Danny Doogood always says: 'New day. New possibility.'"

"What does that have to do with anything?"

"We're starting a new agency. We should use a new bench. I think it will get people's attention."

I do not care one bit what Danny Doogood thinks. I want to sit on the bench I know and love. The bench our clients expect!

But Milton is still walking toward the *other* bench. And *he* has the sign. I have no choice but to follow. Which feels about as pleasant as using someone else's toothbrush. Moxie McCoy *does not follow*!

When I get to the bench I do not want to sit on, Milton pulls out a button and pins it to my coat.

While I sit there trying not to love the button as much as I do, I notice that a bunch of kids are pointing at the sign and saying things like "Excellent motto!" and "I had no idea you guys were detectives!" and "What an excellent bench!"

Milton grins at me. He's too excited to say *I told you so.*

Should we open for business?

MOXIE & milton INC.

UNITED WE STAND
★ ★ ★
JUSTICE WE DEMAND

The crowd of kids looks at us eagerly, and I have no choice but to let this thing happen.

MOXIE and Milton, Inc. is now open for business,

I say.

One at a time, please.

First in line is Lego Macintosh, a third grader with

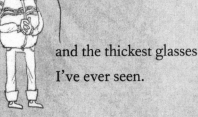

curly red hair,

a billion freckles,

and the thickest glasses
I've ever seen.

It's obvious he has no idea how this is supposed to work
because he stands there with his mouth a little bit open
and doesn't say a word.

What seems to be the problem?

asks Milton.

This is an **OUTRAGEOUS** breach of protocol!

Excuse me,
I say.
But the proper question is
"What seems to be the *issue*?"

Milton looks at me like a dentist who just found out you
haven't been flossing.

We don't know that
Lego has a "problem,"

I explain.

75

Of course, the real *problem* is that Milton spoke first. I make a note to *talk to him about this later.*

Even if we're technically partners, I'm the *lead* partner.

A problem is a *kind* of issue, says Milton.

While I think about that, Lego raises his hand.

Are you guys done?

Yes,

Milton and I both say at the same time.

I make a note to *remind him that I will be the partner that answers every question.*

What seems to be the issue . . . or problem?

I ask, covering my bases.

"It's tragic," says Lego. "My one-by-two light blue Lego hinge brick is missing. I've looked everywhere. And I need it to complete the scale model Hypsilophodon I've been working on."

"Hipsowhatserfungle?" I say.

"Hypsilophodon," says Milton. "An ornithopod dinosaur from the Early Cretaceous. Am I right, Lego?"

"Indeed you are, Milton."

I make a note to talk to Milton about never showing off his superior knowledge of dinosaurs in front of clients.

"So, can you help me?" asks Lego.

I look at Milton. Clearly, he wants to say something, but for the moment he's waiting for me to go first. I consider this is progress.

"When is the last time you saw it?"

"Who can say?" says Lego. "I'm a busy guy. I know I used to have one. And now I need it. I'm willing to hire you, but I expect results."

"Do you suspect foul play?" asks Milton.

It's an excellent question. I am reminded that Milton can sometimes be useful.

"It's possible," says Lego. "I have lots of enemies."

It's true. I don't know anyone who likes Lego very much.

"Well? Will you take the case or not?"

I am tempted to say yes, but then I look at the line of kids waiting to talk to us. A missing Lego is not up to my standards. Plus, as far as I can tell, it might involve the unpleasantness of going to Lego's house and

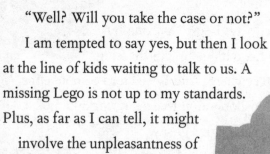

LOOKING UNDER HIS BED.

"I'm afraid that won't be—"

But Milton cuts me off. "If you will allow me to speak with my *partner* for a moment," he says, pulling me over to a nearby tree.

Lego lets out a loud, disgusted sigh to make it clear that if there were any other problem-solving detective duo on the playground, he would definitely take his dollar to them instead.

Milton squints at me as sternly as he can. "If I may remind you of bylaw #4,

'Moxie won't accept or turn down any cases without talking to Milton.'"

Ugh! The bylaws!

Listen, he says. This one's easy.

How's that?

I have the same Lego at home. I'll bring it tomorrow.

Milton tries his hardest to wink at me.

I do not wink back. But I see his point. If Milton is willing to give up his Lego, I'm happy to pocket the dollar and consider another case closed.

I turn back to Lego. "We'll take your case. But we demand payment up front."

Lego digs in his pocket and pulls out a bunch of coins and a few Legos. He hands me three quarters, three nickels, and a dime.

"I'll take that," says Milton.

"*I'll* take it," I say, slightly louder and three times meaner.

Lego makes the right decision.

I slide the money into my pocket, liking how it feels and not much enjoying the thought of giving half of it away.

Milton gives me a glare as he takes out his notebook and writes

OWED TO MILTON

50¢!!

as loudly as I've heard someone write in my whole entire life.

Next up is a first grader named Gwen who says she's been sad ever since her salamander, Mike, died. She wants us to reverse time so she can go back and see him again.

I'm considering taking the case and seeing if Milton can invent a

TIME MACHINE

with all his wires and such, but instead he gives Gwen a hug and suggests she might feel better if she spends a few moments thinking about baby sloths. Gwen closes her eyes and smiles.

Thanks! It worked!

she says before wandering back toward the swing set.

"Technically, you solved her problem," I say.

"I know. Isn't that great?"

"Technically, Gwen owes us a dollar."

"I'm happy to do that one for free."

"Well, *I'm* not. Since you solved that case on agency time, you can give me the money I would have earned if we'd charged her like we should have." I grab Milton's notebook and cross out

Milton does not like this one bit. And I do not care one bit.

"You're acting like Rex," he says, not very nicely.

I scowl at Milton. He scowls at me. We move to opposite ends of the bench.

The *one and only* interesting thing about the Danny Doogood books is Rex Rotten, a kid who lives across the street from Danny and is his opposite in every way.

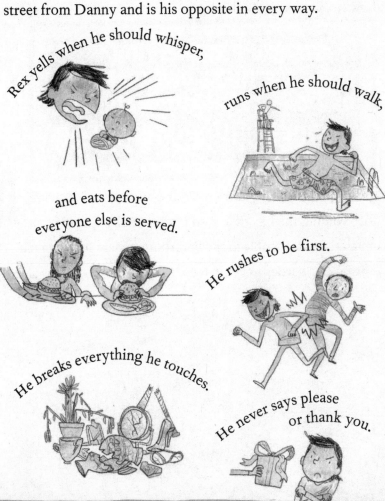

Rex yells when he should whisper,

runs when he should walk,

and eats before everyone else is served.

He rushes to be first.

He breaks everything he touches.

He never says please or thank you.

Rex drives Danny up a wall.
Which is why I like him so much.

A boy named Ichabod is next in line. He's already lost two Owl Points this morning and wants advice on how to avoid losing a third.

EVERYONE KNOWS THAT IF YOU LOSE THREE OWL POINTS IN ONE DAY IT'S AN AUTOMATIC TRIP TO SEE PRINCIPAL JONES.

I tell Ichabod my top-secret-and-time-tested strategy for avoiding the loss of a third Owl Point by spending as much time as possible in the bathroom, where it's so much harder to get in trouble.

Great idea! he says.

But not so much time that you lose an Owl Point for spending *too* much time in the bathroom.

How much is too much?

What grade are you in?

Fifth.

"So . . . Mr. Wiggins. I'd say you can spend about NINE MINUTES in the bathroom at a time without losing an Owl Point."

Do you have a watch?

Yep.

Excellent. Good luck.

I hold out my hand.

Ichabod hands me a dollar.

"See how that works?" I say to Milton.

Milton writes in his notebook Owed to Milton— 50¢

This goes on for a while. We are in demand! But there's no excitement. No intrigue. No shattered mirrors or wailing orphans or twice-cursed artifacts.

I'm looking around for anyone who might be screaming or bleeding when I notice Emily waiting patiently near the end of the line. I wave her to the front.

No fair! says Chaz Danson.

I give him a peppermint, and he simmers down.

Emily!

Moxie!

We do our secret handshake. Everyone says, *Oooooh!*
"I've come for an update. Have you guys made any progress?"

We haven't, of course, because Milton has been distracting us with boring kid stuff. Now that Emily is here, it's time we got down to world-saving. I turn to the crowd.

Thank you for your interest, but we're not taking any more cases today.

Milton clears his throat.

If that's okay with my *partner* . . .

The word tastes as good as a leaky battery.

It is, says Milton. He turns to the crowd.

We'll be back the same time tomorrow.

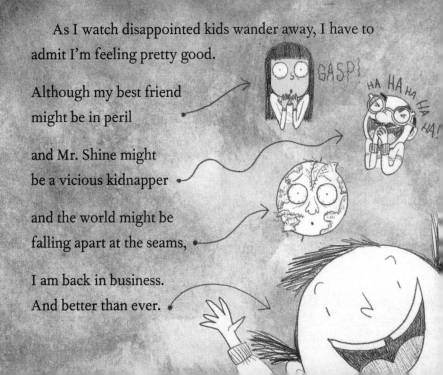

As I watch disappointed kids wander away, I have to admit I'm feeling pretty good.

Although my best friend might be in peril

GASP!

HA HA HA HA HA!

and Mr. Shine might be a vicious kidnapper

and the world might be falling apart at the seams,

I am back in business. And better than ever.

CHAPTER 7: MAKING A PLAN

Emily joins us
on the bench.

"Let's review the facts," I say. "We have no idea where
the Squiggler is now."

"But we do know where the Squiggler *was*," says Milton.
"At Emily's mailbox."

"Precisely," I say. "Precisely" is what Annabelle Adams
says whenever she needs a little more time to find the
solution to a problem she's pretending she already solved.

The *precisely* does its job.

Suddenly,
my brain unleashes
a furious backflip.

We need to have a stakeout!

A stakeout? asks Emily.

A stakeout! We will climb the tree in Emily's yard and secretly observe her mailbox 24 hours a day, seven days a week, 365 days a year until the Squiggler returns. At which point, we'll drop a net on his head and remove his mask!

Or *her* head.

Twenty-four hours a day?

Does the Squiggler have a mask?

Seven days a week?

How did you know I have a tree in my yard?

365 days a year?

"It's true. The Squiggler *could* be a she," I admit. "And whether a *he* or *she*, it seems almost 100% likely that the Squiggler *does* wear a mask. Emily, most yards have trees. It's just a fact. And yes, Milton, to catch the Squiggler, we must be vigilant, even if it means camping out in Emily's tree until we're 18."

"Why will you give up when you turn 18?" says Emily.

"At that point, I'll need to climb down and exercise my civic duty to VOTE."

Good point, says Milton.

Of course, says Emily, who is a big fan of civic duty.

We don't have a moment to waste.

I'm tempted to sprint over to Emily's house at this very moment, but I'm afraid that Principal Jones's secretary, Mrs. Breath (rhymes with *death*), would tackle me with her teeth and drag me back by my ankles.

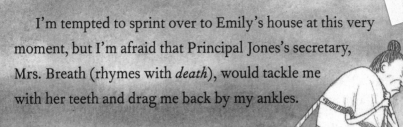

What time do your two dads get home from work?

Usually around 6:00.

Perfect, we should be able to get to your house by 3:20, which means we'll have almost three hours to observe your mailbox before they get home and wonder why there are two strange kids hanging out in their tree.

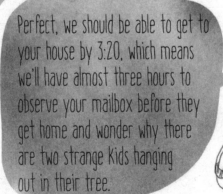

Milton tugs on my arm. "May I please speak to you privately?"

"Certainly. If you will excuse us, Emily, I need to consult with my . . . *partner.*"

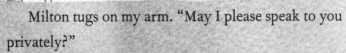

Milton and I go back over to the tree. "What is it?" I am trying not to sound as annoyed as I feel.

"We need to be home by 5:30!"

Milton is not wrong. That's when our one dad gets home from work.

"I am assuming we'll have the Squiggler

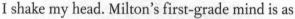

long before then."

"*And* we're not supposed to ride the bus."

"But you are allowed to ride on the bus *if* you have a note from your dad explaining your very good reasons for doing so."

"How can Dad write us a note?"

I shake my head. Milton's first-grade mind is as innocent as a

"*I'll* write the note," I say. "Don't worry."

But Milton is a

"This is what being a detective is all about. I thought you were ready."

Milton looks wounded.

"Fine," I say. "You don't have to come."

"But . . ." Milton is stuck. I'm not *making* him come, but he wants me to want him to be there.

He straightens his glasses and puffs out his chest like a wet baby chick that just broke free of its shell.

I'll come.

Good.

Good.

I walk back over to Emily. "We'll ride home with you after school."

"Oh, hooray! Thanks, you guys."

There's one more thing. I look at Milton. It's not a look he likes.

What do you need me to do?

I need *you* to write the note from Dad.

Milton turns **WHITE.**

I can't! I won't!

Your handwriting looks way more like Dad's.

It's true, and Milton can't deny it.
He gets the look of someone who knows
he has to have his tonsils removed and is
trying to have a good attitude about it.

Fine. What should I write?

"To whom it may concern."

Milton gives me a look.

That's how grown-ups begin every letter.

It sounds weird.

Who is writing this letter?

Fine.

I have a look. It's almost perfect.

"Fine," says Milton, changing the spelling from ~~they're~~ to there. "Shouldn't there be a period somewhere?"

"There is! At the end."

"I mean somewhere else. That's a really LONG sentence."

"It's a beautiful sentence. Some might even call it Magnificent."

Milton says nothing. He shakes his head and says nothing again.

"I wonder if you should *also* be the one to give it to Mrs. Breath."

"Not a chance," says Milton.

And he's right.

Milton would never be able to walk up to Mrs. Breath's desk without crumbling like a cracker in the pocket of your jeans.

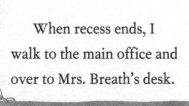

When recess ends, I walk to the main office and over to Mrs. Breath's desk.

Excuse me, Mrs. Breath. Your shoes. I *really* like them.

Of course I cannot see her shoes. They are on her feet, beneath her desk. But Mom always says you can't go wrong complimenting a lady's shoes.

But Mrs. Breath doesn't bite. She doesn't blink. She stares at me the way a bullfrog might stare at a fly that just landed on the wrong lily pad.

What can I do for you, Moxie?

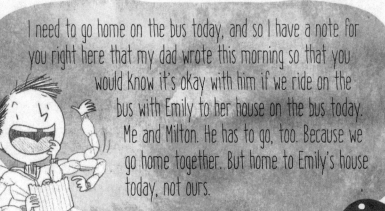

I need to go home on the bus today, and so I have a note for you right here that my dad wrote this morning so that you would know it's okay with him if we ride on the bus with Emily to her house on the bus today. Me and Milton. He has to go, too. Because we go home together. But home to Emily's house today, not ours.

I hand her the note as casually as one adult might hand another adult an ice cube if the other adult's iced tea wasn't quite cold enough.

Mrs. Breath studies the note as if it were a map of the great secrets of the universe. And then she looks at me with eyes of eternity, and suddenly I realize that Mrs. Breath is a *human lie detector*.

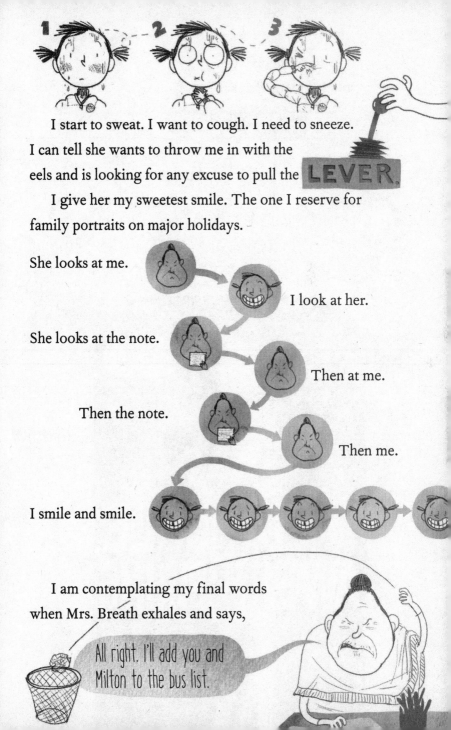

I start to sweat. I want to cough. I need to sneeze. I can tell she wants to throw me in with the eels and is looking for any excuse to pull the LEVER.

I give her my sweetest smile. The one I reserve for family portraits on major holidays.

She looks at me.

I look at her.

She looks at the note.

Then at me.

Then the note.

Then me.

I smile and smile.

I am contemplating my final words when Mrs. Breath exhales and says,

All right. I'll add you and Milton to the bus list.

I stand there, too
stunned to say thanks.

You can go now.

I go. And as I do, I can't help but remind myself,

You are good, Moxie McCoy.
You are really, really good.

But as I'm leaving the office, I hear a familiar voice.

Moxie McCoy.

THERE
SHE
IS.

TALL, NOBLE, AWE-INSPIRING.

Hello, Principal Jones.

"Hello, Moxie. How are things?"

"Things are good. Things are great, in fact. Milton and I have just opened a new detective agency."

"Congratulations. You two make a pretty good team."

"Some would say we're the best in the business."

"Is that so?" Principal Jones raises just one eyebrow in a way that would make Annabelle proud. "Any big cases?"

WELL DONE!

I lean in a little. "It's technically top secret, but because you seem trustworthy, I will tell you that someone sent Emily Estevez an anonymous letter, and we're trying to figure out who."

"How nice!"

I want to tell Principal Jones that it's *not* nice, not even a *little*, but I'm guessing she's never read

Death by Envelope,

so I decide to keep my theory to myself for now.

But I have another concern, and it seems like the perfect moment to bring it up.

"To be honest with you, I fear we're all in

UTMOST DANGER."

Oh? What's going on?

This Mr. Shine character. I'm not sure I trust him.

And why is that?

For one thing, he's so cheerful.

Is that all?

He doesn't even teach us anything. All he does is ask questions!

Mr. Shine's approach is . . . different. It's one of the things I like best about him. Give him some time. I'd be surprised if you don't come to like him quite a bit.

I want to tell Principal Jones she might have hired a dastardly kidnapper, but so far all I have is a hunch and a couple of potential clues. I have learned the hard way that Principal Jones doesn't like it when you accuse someone of

DARK DEEDS WITHOUT IRON🔒CLAD EVIDENCE.

And so I tackle the problem from a different direction. "But what about Mrs. Bunyan? Why would she retire so suddenly?"

"I think Mrs. Bunyan was ready for a break. Did you know that this was her forty-second year at Tiddlywhump?"

"I didn't."

Principal Jones takes down a photograph from the wall of her office. There's a row of young teachers with really strange clothes and even weirder haircuts.

There is someone who looks like she could be Mrs. Bunyan's daughter. Or granddaughter.

But something about her eyes tells me it's actually Mrs. Bunyan herself, though it's hard to tell because she's smiling, which is not on the Mrs. Bunyan knows how to make.

MENU OF FACES

-----$12   -----$10

--UNAVAILABLE   -----$12

-----$10   -----$8

WOW, I say.

For the first time in my life, I see that Mrs. Bunyan

was once a person with

ACTUAL FEELINGS.

Happy ones, even.

Give Mr. Shine a little time, says Principal Jones.

I know you're going to like him. He's one of the good ones.

Back in class, Mr. Shine finally starts teaching us things. *Sort of.* We are talking about the AMERICAN *Revolution* but instead of telling us what happened and who did what and when and why and how and to who, it goes like this:

Mr. Shine asks a question.

Someone gives the wrong answer.

He asks another question that includes some sort of hint.

Someone gives a better answer.

He asks another question with another hint.

Finally, someone gives the right answer,

and Mr. Shine gives a really big smile.

Tracy Dublinger raises her hand.

Wouldn't it be easier to just tell us the answers to begin with?

she asks in an irritated way.

Tracy likes teachers to tell her exactly what she's supposed to know, so she can memorize it and get perfect scores on all her tests.

"It might be *easier*," says Mr. Shine, "but I think an answer means a lot more when you have to find it yourself."

Kind of like solving a mystery, I say.

Exactly, says Mr. Shine.

In a way, students are detectives, and teachers are there to help them find clues.

I like how that sounds, and I'm sitting there flipping it over like a pancake when Bob Tuttleman gets a little too excited and falls out of his chair.

Mr. Shine tells us all to stand up and shake our arms as hard as we can for 30 seconds. Which might be the weirdest thing that has ever happened in the history of the fourth grade. But after that, I have to admit, Bob does bounce up and down a little less than usual.

It is entirely **OUTRAGEOUS** behavior for a teacher, and I consider marching right back to Principal Jones to let her know what's happening. But for the time being, at least, I find myself enjoying it.

CHAPTER 8: THE STAKEOUT

The day ends, but instead of heading to the front of the school, Milton and I go to the back parking lot where the buses line up.

Are you sure about this? says Milton, looking even less certain than usual.

I'm sure.

I give him a wink. We squeeze into a seat with Emily. The Dublingers are on the other side of the bus.

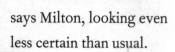

They give me a glare.

I give them a glare.

We play glare tennis.

It goes on for a while.

Eventually, the bus pulls up to a perfect white house with bushes shaped like animals and a statue of a lion on the lawn.

As Tracy leaves the bus, she looks back with one final glare. I give her a dignified nod to let her know I'm ready for any challenge.

A few minutes later, the bus stops again.

Here we are, says Emily.

It is a thrilling moment! My very first visit to my best friend's house! It is a small but friendly-looking place with yellow paint and red shutters and boxes full of flowers in the windows.

Do you guys want a snack before we get started? says Emily.

Sure, says Milton.

Absolutely not! I insist.

Where is the mailbox?

"There," says Emily, pointing.

It's a normal-looking mailbox, though it wobbles a little.

"Is the wobble new?" asks Milton.

"It has always wobbled," says Emily.

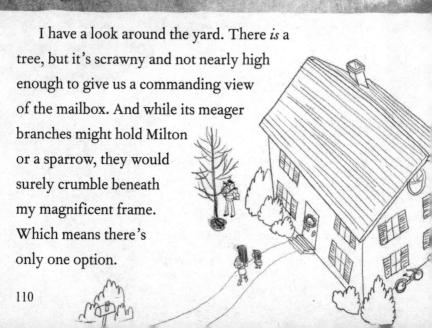

I have a look around the yard. There *is* a tree, but it's scrawny and not nearly high enough to give us a commanding view of the mailbox. And while its meager branches might hold Milton or a sparrow, they would surely crumble beneath my magnificent frame. Which means there's only one option.

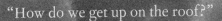

"How do we get up on the roof?"

"The *roof*?" asks Emily.

"Absolutely not," says Milton.

But I am already in motion, into the
house, up the stairs, into the attic

like a bolt of lightning streaking
through the midnight sky above
a desolate mountaintop fortress.

As I suspected, by crawling out
the highest window and grabbing on
to the gutter, we should be able to pull
ourselves onto the roof. I'm halfway
up when Milton shrieks for me to

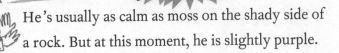

He's usually as calm as moss on the shady side of
a rock. But at this moment, he is slightly purple.

111

"This isn't going to happen." Milton pulls a piece of paper from his pocket. "I'd like to remind you of the document you signed this morning."

I give Milton the look that usually makes him do whatever I say. But today it isn't working.

"Please see bylaw number seven."

"As I recall, there were only six bylaws."

"There," he says, handing me a magnifying glass and pointing to the bottom of the page.

"Look closely."

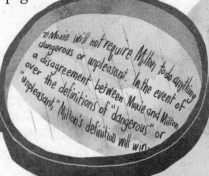

7. Moxie will not require Milton to do anything dangerous or unpleasant. In the event of a disagreement between Moxie and Milton over the definitions of "dangerous" or "unpleasant," Milton's definition will win.

I am shocked and enraged.

HOW DID YOU WRITE THAT SO SMALL?

That's why they call it fine print, says Milton, looking smug.

"BUT IT IS SO INCREDIBLY TINY!!"

"Is that your signature?" he insists.

"I HAVE BEEN DUPED! I HAVE BEEN FOOLED!"

"As Danny Doogood often says, 'If you let someone fool you, *you're* the fool.'"

I am about to say some not-very-sisterly things when I suddenly remember bylaw number one.

"What about

What about it?

"'Milton will be a *full partner*.' Full partners do not cower in the attic while their daring sisters do the dangerous work. Full partners do *not* trick their sisters with sneaky microscopic sentences! What would Danny say about *that*?"

"He would say—"

But Milton stops. He knows full well that Danny would rather swallow a pair of scissors than trick his sister on purpose.

As we stand there glaring
at each other like Dublingers,
Emily looks at us like a sad
deer watching a forest fire.

"I'm going up," I say. "You stay here if you want. It's
perfectly clear you're not ready to be a partner."

I'm halfway out the window when Milton says, "Wait."

He walks over, and I help him up onto the roof.

"Oh my goodness, be careful," says Emily. I give her a
wink and pull myself up.

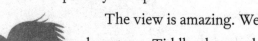

The view is amazing. We can see
downtown Tiddlywhump, the woods,
the water tower, the river.

Even though he's still mad, I can tell that Milton is a little bit thrilled about what's happening. He doesn't usually do anything that isn't boring and safe and predictable. He doesn't usually get a chance to feel so tall.

One thing is certain: We have an excellent view of the mailbox. I assume the Squiggler will show up at any moment.

We wait. And wait. A man walks down the sidewalk wearing a hooded sweatshirt.

"Extremely suspicious!" I say.

"If only we had a big net," says Milton.

But the man walks right past Emily's mailbox.

Two teenage girls walk by, chatting about this or that.

"Could one of them be the Squiggler?"

"I think it's the one on the right," says Milton.

They walk on by.

Eventually, someone *does* walk straight up to the mailbox. A man in a blue shirt with a bag over his shoulder!

We've got him! I say.

That's the mailman, says Milton.

Milton is not wrong. And so we wait. And wait.

"You haven't said even one nice thing about me today,"
says Milton, referring, of course, to **BYLAW #5.**

That may be true, but technically, I still have plenty of
time left.

"*I will*," I say. And I will. As soon as I think of something.

IT STARTS TO RAIN

Milton looks at his watch.

I don't think the Squiggler is coming.

But he could show up at any moment.

I'm getting wet.

I say nothing. I am staring at the mailbox and focusing
on not blinking in case the Squiggler is lightning-fast.

WHERE IS EVERYONE?

"Dad's going to be home soon," says Milton.

"Are you committed to solving this mystery or not?"

"Of course I am."

"Prove it."

"You're doing it again."

"What?"

"Acting like Rex."

"Rex is a rowdy seven-year-old who never washes his hands and chews with his mouth open. *I am a professional!*"

"Rex is thoughtless and rude," says Milton. "Rex doesn't care if he's late for dinner or puts other people in dangerous situations. Danny would say that this roof is getting slippery and that it's going to be dark soon and that we can try to catch the Squiggler tomorrow."

Stop acting like DANNY DOOGOOD! We are in the middle of a stakeout!

By and by, mutters Milton under his breath.

What did you say?

But I know what he said.

"By and by" is what Danny says to calm himself down when he's frustrated with Rex. Which means he says it a lot.

Danny's entire purpose in life—his REASON FOR BEING ALIVE —is trying to convince Rex to be as good and perfect as Danny.

As I was reading Book 1: *Doing Good*, I found myself cheering for Rex every time he did something awful. I kept waiting for Danny to get frustrated and yell at Rex or give up on him, but DANNY NEVER DOES! Instead, he says "By and by" and keeps patiently showing Rex the right way to do things. Eventually, at the very end of Book 1, Rex finally does something right and says,

Now I see you're right, Danny. It is better to do good.

DANNY DOOGOOD

I read that sentence and screamed and threw the book across the room and broke my orange juice glass and vowed that I will never, ever read another Danny Doogood book as long as I live.

If being Milton's partner means getting battered with constant advice from Danny, I'm not interested.

You and your do-gooding self can get off this roof and help a thousand old ladies cross the street a thousand times. I'm going to stay up here and save the world.

Fine,

says Milton.

I'm going. But first I want my 50 cents.

What? 119

Carefully keeping one hand on the roof, Milton uses his other hand to pull out his notebook and shows me the page that says:

OWED TO MILTON 50¢!!

I am flabbergasted. This is no time to think about money! This is a time to be 200% FOCUSED on catching the Squiggler.

"I'll give you your 50 cents as soon as you start acting like a partner instead of a do-gooding sidekick!"

Milton looks at me with rage. I am afraid he's going to leap across the rooftop and bite me in the ankle.

That's a violation of bylaw #3! You agreed to never call me *sidekick!*

Maybe Milton is right, but I do not like bylaw #3. And now that I've violated it, I decide to go all in.

 "How about *lackey*, then?"

"I would stop right now if I were you. As Danny Doogood would say, 'Words have consequences!'"

"What a GNOMISH thing to say!"

Milton is madder than a bee that has just been stung by seven other bees.

I AM NOT YOUR SIDEKICK! OR A LACKEY! I AM NOT GNOMISH! I AM YOUR PARTNER! AND *I* WANT MY 50 CENTS!

I have never seen Milton this angry before. And I know I should back down. But I can't stop myself.

"Don't you mean 'by and by' . . . *Danny*?" I say, digging two quarters out of my pocket and

tossing them in his general direction.

But because Milton is using both of his hands to hold on, the quarters bounce off his chest and start skittering down the roof, which upsets one half of Milton's brain so much that he lunges to catch them

before the other half realizes that this is a terrible idea.

ERP! says Milton as he starts to slide down the roof.

I catch his hand and manage to stop him for just a piece of a second, but the roof is steep, and Milton's wet fingers slip right through mine.

His eyes get as wide as two planets as he shoots backward on his belly down the roof and disappears over the edge.

I hear a CRASH and an "OOF"

and then

silence.

My heart stops. I climb back through the window and race downstairs and out to the lawn. Emily is already there. Milton is nowhere to be seen. There is a first-grader-sized dent in the bush by the front door. I peer into the bush.

MILTON!

No answer.

"Are you in there? I'm so sorry! Please say something!"

"Oh my goodness! Oh my goodness!" says Emily. I have to say, she's not being particularly helpful.

I finally conclude that Milton is not in the bush. But where could he be? I look around the yard. I look up and down the street. No Milton. "Can I borrow your bike?" I ask.

"Of course!" says Emily.

I ride around the neighborhood calling Milton's name and saying how sorry I am, but he's nowhere to be found.

I get back to Emily's house just as a car pulls into the driveway. Emily is doing a terrible job trying to look calm as a tall and friendly-looking man gets out of the car.

"Moxie, this is my dad."

"Pleased to meet you," I say.

"And you," he says, shaking my hand. "I'm Jim."

"When's Dad coming home?" says Emily to her dad.

"In a few minutes," says the dad who is already there. "He's getting some groceries."

I'd like to stand there chatting, but I'm extremely worried about Milton.

"Could you give Moxie a ride home?" asks Emily.

"Sure," says Jim.

"See you tomorrow," says Emily, giving me a hug. "And let me know when you find Milton," she whispers in my ear.

I get into the car. We pull out of the driveway.

All I can think about is Milton, but I don't really want to explain to Jim that I just let my little brother slide off his roof, and so I try to come up with some pleasant chitchat.

So ... you're one of Emily's *two* dads?

127

"I am," says Jim. He seems really happy about it. As I would be. You couldn't ask for a better daughter.

"I observed that Emily calls you Dad," I say.

"She does."

"And that she also calls her other dad, Dad?"

"That's right."

"Doesn't that get confusing?"

"Not usually," he says. "Sometimes, I guess."

"That must be a lot of work for Emily on Father's Day."

Jim smiles. "She seems to manage."

Suddenly, I'm full of questions, such as

But where is Emily's mom?

and *Who does Emily bring to school on Bring Your Mom to School Day?*

and *How does Emily get by without an admirable female scientist role model in her life?*

128

But I'm not exactly sure whether it would be impolite to ask these things, and so I sit there looking out the window. Jim asks me about my family, but I'm too worried to come up with any pleasant chitchat.

Jim pulls into my driveway.

Thanks for the ride.

No problem. I hope you'll come visit Emily again soon.

I definitely will.

It's 5:25. Fortunately, Dad is not home yet. I race inside and RUSH UPSTAIRS.

Milton's bedroom door is closed, but I know he's in there because I can see light through the crack at the bottom and because there is a sign that says:

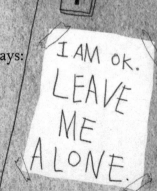

I AM OK. LEAVE ME ALONE.

I have visions of Milton lying on the ground with two broken legs and two broken arms, writing the sign with a pen held between his teeth. I need to make sure he's really okay.

Are you really okay?

I say to the door.

Read the sign.

I did. I just wanted to make sure you were really REALLY and truly okay.

Read the sign.

I'm really, really sorry. Are you 150% sure you're okay?

READ.
THE.
SIGN.

I decide that anyone who can yell so loud is probably fine. It also seems clear that Milton has no interest in continuing the conversation.

I let out all the breath inside me and collapse onto my bed in sheer relief.

A few minutes later, I hear the garage door and go down and give Dad a big hug.

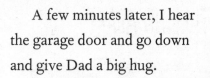

And then I eat a sandwich and go to bed,

saying I have lots of homework (true)

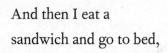

and that I'm not feeling well (half true).

Mostly, though, I can't stand the thought of looking Milton in the eye.

CHAPTER 9: FALLING APART

There's another envelope
waiting on my place mat the
next morning. Milton is sitting
there reading a book called

History's
Great
Treacherous
Acts.

OW.

He doesn't look at me.

I open the envelope and notice another beautiful border.
And another gold seal. My heart leaps! Perhaps Milton
has created an extremely
attractive apology for being
so careless and sliding
off the roof. But then
I take a closer look
and realize that
something very
different is
happening.

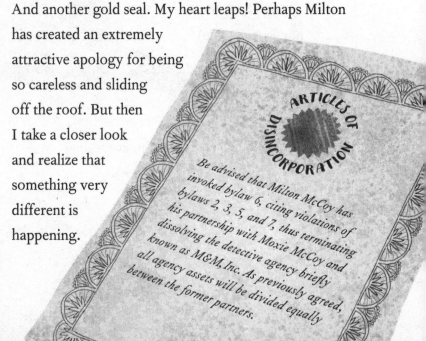

ARTICLES OF
DISINCORPORATION

Be advised that Milton McCoy has
invoked bylaw 6, citing violations of
bylaws 2, 3, 5, and 7, thus terminating
his partnership with Moxie McCoy and
dissolving the detective agency briefly
known as M&M, Inc. As previously agreed,
all agency assets will be divided equally
between the former partners.

I'd be worried if this weren't such a funny joke. I look at Milton, expecting him to laugh.

He does not laugh.

"What's going on?" I ask.

"I am done," says Milton without looking up.

"Look, I'm really sorry about last night, but these things sometimes happen."

"I am *done*."

"But we're just getting started!"

This time he looks up. This is not the Milton I have known for six and a half years. This is a lion that has just escaped from the zoo and is ready to gobble some tourists.

Milton holds out his hand.

All agency assets will be divided equally.

I'm not sure what you're—

YOU OWE ME FIFTY CENTS!

But I gave—

YOU OWE ME FIFTY CENTS!

Milton stands up. He looks surprisingly menacing.

All the fight goes out of me.
I dig into my pocket.

Here,

I say,

handing him two quarters.

Milton takes the money and sits back down.

136

Dad comes in, looking concerned.

What's going on?

Nothing, I say.

Nothing, says Milton.

I thought I heard shouting.

I was practicing for kickball, I say, thinking fast.

Research shows the ball goes much farther if you yell really loudly right when you kick it.

Is that so? asks Dad.

100%, absolutely, I say.

Dad smiles and shakes his head and pours himself some coffee. And I am 100%, absolutely glad we don't have to get into the real reason Milton and I were yelling at each other.

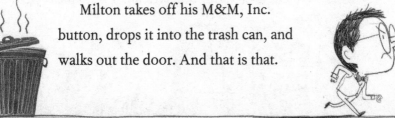

Milton takes off his M&M, Inc. button, drops it into the trash can, and walks out the door. And that is that.

Milton walks half a block behind me all the way to school. I hope he's able to work out whatever is bothering him by recess, because it will be awkward talking to clients if we're still fighting.

At school, the hallway is filled with excited chattering. I overhear Kate Johnson talking to Samaara Patil in the whispery, hard-to-hear voices they always use.

... found a mysterious letter.

Where?

In his backpack, yesterday afternoon.

Who was it from?

It wasn't signed!

Who was it to again?

A first grader named John.

Never heard of him.

But *I've* heard of him. Milton's friend. The hapless victim

in the
CASE of the
MISSING
BALL.

If the Squiggler has truly struck again, it's essential that I get to John before Milton does. But John is nowhere to be seen. And so I listen carefully to what everyone is saying. As it turns out, there's plenty of information swirling around.

"... full of really nice compliments ..."

"... had a purple squiggle on the envelope ..."

"... from 'the person he least expects'!"

I spend so much time reading lips and taking notes that I'm the last one into Mr. Shine's classroom. As I slide into my seat in the

VALLEY OF THE SHADOW OF DUBLINGER,

I glance across the room at Emily. She waves as pleasantly as a sunflower on a bright summer day.

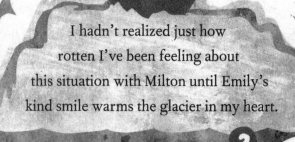

I hadn't realized just how rotten I've been feeling about this situation with Milton until Emily's kind smile warms the glacier in my heart.

Mr. Shine is wearing suspenders today. Orange ones. He sort of halfway teaches us a thing or two about commas but mostly just asks questions.

I do not see his pink hat.

He does not refer to his noggin.

I am not yet entirely convinced that he is a kidnapping criminal mastermind, but I am not entirely unconvinced, either.

When the recess bell rings, I race out to the playground and look for John. I am in luck! There he is, and Milton doesn't seem to have found him yet.

"John!" I say, throwing my arm around him as if he were the peanut butter side of a sandwich and I am his jelly.

"Of course! Old pals, you and me. I hear you got a mysterious letter."

"Um."

"I bet you'd like to know who it's from."

"Actually, I—"

I grab John by the shoulders, put my face really close to his, and give him a smile the size of an avalanche.

"THIS IS YOUR LUCKY DAY, JOHN. I'm offering a discount today *and today only*! I'll figure out who sent you that letter for ONLY 50 CENTS."

John looks at me and then at the ground, and then over to the far bench, where Milton is sitting with a pair of binoculars, watching our every move.

"Milton said he'd take my case for free."
I think quick.

"When I said 50 cents, I meant I'd pay YOU 50 cents, John! For the *honor* of working on your case. What do you say?"

John looks at me as if I were a madwoman, and I realize I'm probably talking louder than I need to.

"Ireallyhavetogonowbye."

I watch as John scurries over, sits next to Milton, and pulls something out of his pocket.

I watch as Milton takes a close look at whatever it is.

I watch as Milton turns his head and looks at me and smiles.

I recognize the smile.
It's the smile that Dr. Fungo
uses in Volume 1:

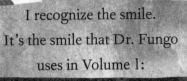

MEET ANNABELLE ADAMS

right before he commands 99 laser-hand robots to
incinerate Annabelle's asthmatic friend, Floyd.

It's the smile you'd use to let your nemesis know you've just
discovered the *exact* piece of evidence you need to identify
the Squiggler.

It suddenly occurs to me that I am Milton's nemesis.
Which isn't something I feel great about.

I walk over to my old bench. There on the seat is one
half of a sign.

I am sitting there feeling extremely sorry for myself when I see the only person who could possibly cheer me up.

Emily reaches out her elbow to begin our secret handshake, but I just don't have it in me.

I think about how much I need a hug. But before I can ask for a hug, Emily gives me one.

"And now Milton has the *exact piece of evidence* we need to identify the Squiggler!"

"I guess I'd better go talk to him, then."

It's as if Emily has told me she's about to share a slice of pizza with a werewolf.

145

WE MATE FOR LIFE!

For some reason, Emily doesn't seem
to understand that because she and I are
the best of friends, as inseparable and
endlessly loyal as two prairie voles,
any bad thing that happens to me has also
happened to her. I'm trying to figure out
the best way to explain this when she says,

I can Kind of see his side of things, actually.

I feel like a sand castle that is trapped between a
tidal wave and a rampaging two-year-old.

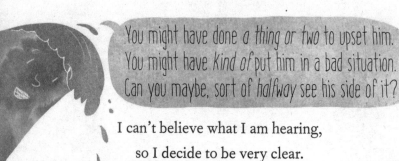

You might have done *a thing or two* to upset him.
You might have *kind of* put him in a bad situation.
Can you maybe, sort of *halfway* see his side of it?

I can't believe what I am hearing,
so I decide to be very clear.

Emily, let me be very clear. If you go over there
and talk to Milton, the greatest friendship in the
history of friendships will be in serious jeopardy.

146

Emily's smile turns into something I don't recognize.

"I'm really sorry you feel that way." She looks down at her knees, then turns and walks away.

I watch as Emily joins Milton and John on the other bench. I watch as Milton hands John's letter to Emily. I watch as Emily says something and the three of them laugh about whatever it was.

I feel like the last green bean that gets left on your tray at the end of lunch because you're already full. The one that gets scraped into the trash as you walk out the door.

My bench has never seemed lonelier.

I glance over to where the Dublingers should be playing tetherball. Tammy is standing there all alone, practicing her half of the Dublinger secret handshake.

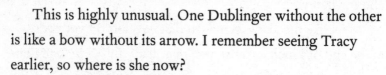

This is highly unusual. One Dublinger without the other is like a bow without its arrow. I remember seeing Tracy earlier, so where is she now?

I'd like to get Milton's take. But he and John and Emily are still chatting and laughing and saving the world without me.

When I get back to class, Tracy is still not there. Mr. Shine has just started asking us questions about pronouns when she walks in and takes her seat—

WITHOUT EVEN SHOWING HER HALL PASS!!!!

I keep an eye on Tracy, who is busy writing down each and every word that comes out of Mr. Shine's mouth. Of course she has perfect penmanship, and I watch with secret admiration as her pencil flies neatly across the page.

But something is not right. Tracy's right hand, which is usually as clean and pink and spotless as a bishop's candelabra, is covered with . . . PURPLE SMUDGES.

Could it be—my heart lunges at the possibility—that Tracy spent recess *writing a letter with a purple squiggle on the envelope*? It is a delicious hunch, but I need proof. And I will find it.

I decide *not* to glance over at Emily. Of course, I want to know if she's glancing over at me. Eventually, I glance just the tiniest glance, and when I do, I see Emily smiling at me as longingly as a cat on the wrong side of a river.

While I try to decide whether I should smile back, I think of Annabelle Adams, who once burned every last photograph of her best friend, Eleanor, to erase the painful memories after Eleanor ran off in a treacherous rage and joined forces with Annabelle's nemesis, Dr. Fungo, on the

Island of Miniature Porcupines.

But I do not have any photographs
of Emily Estevez, and even if I did, I
probably wouldn't burn them because
she is so kind and pure and admirable. At
least she *was* . . . until she shattered my
soul with an act of unthinkable betrayal.

I make up my mind. I do not smile back.
In fact, I even scowl a little.

Emily makes a face like the Tooth
Fairy might when she hears some kid
doesn't believe in her anymore.

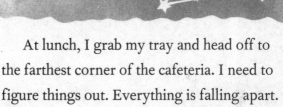

At lunch, I grab my tray and head off to
the farthest corner of the cafeteria. I need to
figure things out. Everything is falling apart.

I've made no progress on the case. I have no access to the critical evidence. My partner won't talk to me (in fact, he won't even look at me). And my best friend has betrayed me.

I am tempted to drop the case and quit school and herd cattle on the Pampas of Argentina, but I am reminded of the time in Volume 38: *Seal of Approval* when the princess of North Gargantua asks Annabelle to save a pod of stranded baby seals, but then it turns out the princess is actually Dr. Fungo's demented niece Margo in disguise and the seals are just an elaborate smoke screen to keep Annabelle distracted while Fungo's robot army steals the enormous bronze hamburger from the sculpture of Lord Much, a plot that Annabelle figures out instantly and squashes single-handedly because she's just that good.

Does Annabelle return the hamburger and go back to her condominium and sit in her hot tub and eat a bunch of cheesecake?

OF COURSE NOT.

Because even though Margo is a sneaky fraud, those stranded seals still need saving!

With or without Milton, with or without Emily, I will unmask the Squiggler and save the day.

Because SOMEBODY has to.

I'm trying to make sense of it all when I feel a gentle hand on my shoulder.

It's Emily, looking like a puppy stuck in a rainstorm. My heart leaps. But I do not let it show.

"What?" I say.

I'm sorry, she says. I didn't mean to hurt your feelings.

My heart **EXPLODES** like the finale of a fireworks show.

MY Life WithoUt Emily EsteveZ was a cold, sad wasteland full of empty bottles and broken dreams. Now she's here and we can get back to business.

That's okay.

I extend my elbow, and she extends hers, and we have perhaps the most satisfying secret handshake of our already extraordinary friendship.

Emily sits down across the table and looks at me with the love of a hundred baby unicorns.

> Do you understand why I went over to talk to Milton?

I can't say that I do, exactly, but I'm not interested in dragging us back into the past. Emily and I are best friends again and will be forever, and that is all that matters.

> Of course.

> So we're okay?

I reach both of my hands out to Emily. It's a thing I've seen girls do on TV shows, and I want to see how it feels. Emily takes my hands. We look into each other's eyes. It's even better than banana cream pie with actual banana slices on top.

I have an idea.

Emily, can we make a promise to never fight again and to always be completely honest with each other and to always tell each other everything?

Sure!

Great!

I consider taking out a piece of paper and writing some

Best Friend Bylaws

so that both of us will always know exactly what is and isn't okay to do or think or say at any given moment. But I don't, because it seems like something Danny would do, and I feel like kicking Danny in the shin.

Plus, bylaws are unnecessary when it comes to a friendship like ours.

We are sitting there together, chewing and smiling like best friends do, saying not much of anything, when a thrilling thought slams into my brain like a big-fisted giant pounding on a flimsy wooden door.

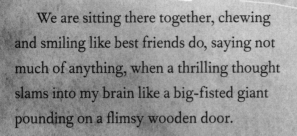

Best friends tell each other everything!

"Tell me everything!"

"What do you mean?"

"John's letter! Milton's theories and observations! Tell me everything you learned about the case! About the Squiggler! You have *all the information* we need!"

Emily's nose and forehead fill with wrinkles. "I'm sorry, but Milton asked me not to talk about the case. He said those things were *top secret*."

I look at Emily as seriously as a doctor looks at a GUSHING WOUND!

"Emily. Let's back up for just a second. Are you my friend?"

"Of course!"

"Good. I just wanted to be sure. Next point. Did we or did we not just promise to never fight and to be honest with each other and to *tell each other everything*?"

Emily lets that sink in.

"All of that is true. But I made a promise to Milton."

"What about your promise to *me*?"

Emily looks like the rope in a tug-of-war.

"I *don't* want to fight, and I *am* being honest, and I'll tell you everything *except* when it means breaking a promise I've made to someone else."

"So . . . let me get this straight . . . you're picking Milton over me? *Again?*"

"It's an impossible situation!"

"You think Milton's secrets are more important than our friendship?"

"They're *equally* important!"

"This is your last chance to save what might be the greatest friendship in the history of friendships."

"I'm sorry, but I just can't—!"

This lunch is over, I say.

And for the record, you've sided with the wrong McCoy.

OUCH!

Emily looks like a soda can that has just been run over by a dump truck full of cinder blocks. If she were still my best friend, I'd give her a long, encouraging hug.

But she isn't.   So I don't.

Instead, I walk off in a huff. But since I have nowhere to go until lunch ends, I spend the next fifteen minutes alone in the bathroom, not losing Owl Points while practicing my single eyebrow lift.

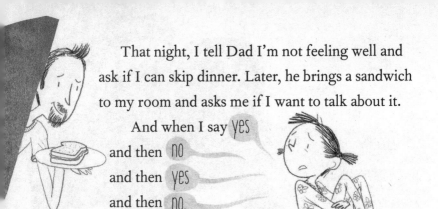

That night, I tell Dad I'm not feeling well and ask if I can skip dinner. Later, he brings a sandwich to my room and asks me if I want to talk about it.

And when I say yes
and then no
and then yes
and then no,

he gives me two hugs and asks if maybe I'd like to talk to Mom.

And I would. More than anything in the world.

But instead we get Mom's voice mail, which says that she's gone on a weeklong trek beyond cell phone range. I picture her on her raft, alone with nothing but a paddle in piranha-infested waters, bravely dodging ten-foot pythons, accomplishing great feats, and saving the world while she's at it.

Dad gives me a third hug
and sits there for a while,

not really talking but saying exactly what I need to hear.

CHAPTER 10: GATHERING EVIDENCE

The next day at recess, both Milton and I have lines at our benches. Kids wave dollars and demand answers. The Squiggler has been busy.

First up is a fifth grader named DeeDee Washington. Talking to DeeDee is like talking to a helicopter that's trying to take off.

Tell me what happened, DeeDee.

Okay, okay, okay. I found this envelope with MY NAME on it in the pocket of my binder. Inside is a letter addressed to ME, full of REALLY NICE THINGS about ME.

Please calm down, DeeDee. I cannot help you if you won't calm down.

If you say so.

DeeDee sits for about three seconds before bouncing right back up.

BUT I'M TOO EXCITED TO BE CALM!

The envelope is pink. DeeDee's name is written in red marker. Emily's envelope was white, and the writing was done with a black pen. But the purple squiggle is the same.

The Squiggler is a criminal mastermind!

I say as gravely as I can. I need to let DeeDee know that she's probably doomed, but DeeDee isn't having it.

Read the letter. READ IT!

I wish DeeDee would stop telling me how to do my job. I'm almost tempted NOT to read the letter in order to teach her a lesson. But I glance over at Milton's bench. At this very moment, he, too, is talking to clients. He, too, is examining their letters, collecting clues, and drawing conclusions. Every second, he is inching closer to solving the mystery.

Mice do not beat lions.

Snowmen do not get the better of active volcanoes.

Milton McCoy will not crack this case before I do.

HEY!

I open DeeDee's letter and get to work:

Dear DeeDee,
I want you to know how much I appreciate you. You are one of the nicest people I know. I like how you laugh and your hair is great! I also like your pretty purple socks. Where did you get them?

— The Person You'd Least Expect

Thank you, DeeDee. After much deliberation, I have decided to take your case.

YESSSSSSS!

DeeDee hands me a dollar. I am tempted to take it, but I have decided that, due to the importance of this case, I'm going to do it

 which means

which makes me feel like I've been bitten by 1,000 mosquitoes. But when Milton decided not to charge for Squiggler cases, I basically had no choice.

"That won't be necessary, DeeDee."

"Oh my GOODness. Thank you. And you'll tell me AS SOON AS you know who sent it?"

"I will."

"GOOD. Because I REALLY want to thank whoever it was. I want to bake them some COOKIES. I want to let them borrow my PURPLE SOCKS."

It occurs to me that if the Squiggler is within earshot, he *really* won't want his identity revealed now.

DeeDee is so excited that she doesn't seem to realize I still have her letter, and since it might be needed in the trial to put the Squiggler behind bars forever, I decide not to remind her.

Next in line is a third grader named Roy. He hands me his letter.

"Where did you find it?"

"In my lunch box. Was minding my own business. Was getting ready to eat my tuna fish sandwich, and there it was, wedged between my orange and my juice box."

"It sounds like you must have left your lunch box unattended."

I say this with one raised eyebrow to let Roy know he had it coming.

"I left it on the table while I went to the bathroom."

I shake my head. Roy looks sheepish. As he should.

I question Roy. His story is not so different from DeeDee's. And then I talk to Taevon, Julie, Maxine, and Felipe about *their* Squiggler letters.

166

Some patterns emerge:

1. None of the letters have stamps.
2. All of the envelopes have purple squiggles in more or less the same place.
3. Every letter begins with "I want you to know how much I appreciate you."
4. Every letter is signed "The person you'd least expect."

ROY

DeeDee

ED

AMOND

But there are important differences, too:

TAEYON

Emily

MAXINE

ULIE

1. Some are written in pencil and others in **pen**.
2. The handwriting is not always the same.
3. One is written with letters cut out of a magazine, like

RANSOM NOTES

often are.

Felipe

Which makes me wonder if the Squiggler

Marcell

might also be a kidnapper.

As far as I know, there is only one suspected kidnapper at Tiddlywhump Elementary. I think of Mr. Shine and his pink hat and his smoggy noggin.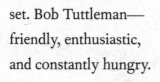

If he's hiding something, I need to find out what it is. If only I could conduct a thorough search of his desk. But that is

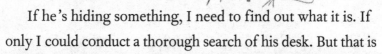

because Mr. Shine is always in his classroom.

Except . . . *at this very minute* . . . during first recess, when he stands outside chatting with the other teachers and making sure we don't run amok.

I glance over at the doors. It would be *extremely difficult* to sneak past the teachers. Unless . . . they happened to be distracted by a sudden crisis.

I look around and spot the very person I'm hoping to see, over by the swing set. Bob Tuttleman— friendly, enthusiastic, and constantly hungry.

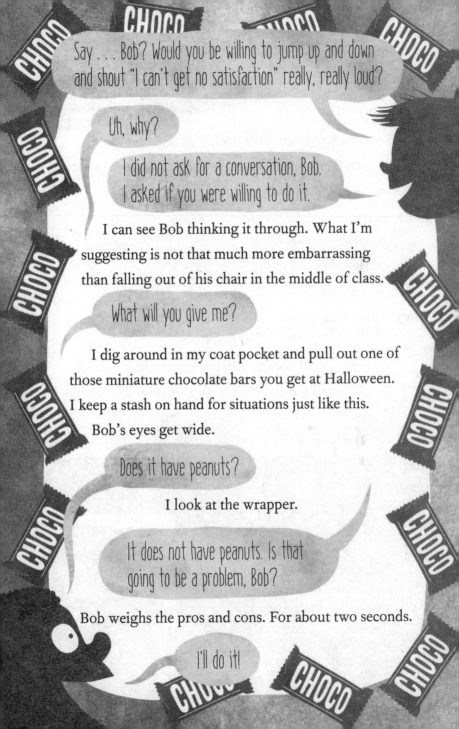

Say . . . Bob? Would you be willing to jump up and down and shout "I can't get no satisfaction" really, really loud?

Uh, why?

I did not ask for a conversation, Bob.
I asked if you were willing to do it.

I can see Bob thinking it through. What I'm suggesting is not that much more embarrassing than falling out of his chair in the middle of class.

What will you give me?

I dig around in my coat pocket and pull out one of those miniature chocolate bars you get at Halloween. I keep a stash on hand for situations just like this. Bob's eyes get wide.

Does it have peanuts?

I look at the wrapper.

It does not have peanuts. Is that going to be a problem, Bob?

Bob weighs the pros and cons. For about two seconds.

I'll do it!

I toss Bob the chocolate,

and he immediately starts bouncing up and down and shouting about satisfaction and how he can't seem to get it. As it turns out, Bob is just as good at yelling as he is at jumping.

The words Bob is shouting are from an old song my dad likes, so I figure the teachers might like it, too.

I CAN'T GET NO OH NO NO NO HEY HEY HEY!

As I'd hoped, they get curious and wander over to see what Bob is up to.

Which makes it easy to slip into the school.

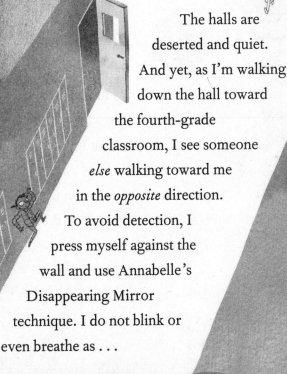

The halls are deserted and quiet. And yet, as I'm walking down the hall toward the fourth-grade classroom, I see someone *else* walking toward me in the *opposite* direction. To avoid detection, I press myself against the wall and use Annabelle's Disappearing Mirror technique. I do not blink or even breathe as . . .

Tracy Dublinger walks right by me and out onto the playground.

I want to get to the bottom of where Tracy has been and what she has been up to, but I only have a few minutes before recess ends. And so I stick to my original plan and hurry down the hall to the fourth-grade classroom.

The lights are off, and the room is empty, and everything looks slightly haunted. I creep to the front of the room and open the supply closet, half expecting to find Mrs. Bunyan tied to a chair with a sock in her mouth.

Instead, I find a shelf full of textbooks, a few coats, and a splintery hockey stick.

I creep over to Mr. Shine's desk. There's nothing on top but the two apples Tammy and Tracy brought for him this morning, so I check the pencil drawer.

But there's nothing out of the ordinary. Just some

pushpins

and some rubber bands,

a handful of pencils,

a paper clip or two,

and a purple marker.

I'm about to shut the drawer when my brain catches up with my eyes.

A PURPLE MARKER!

I pull out my notebook and make a squiggle and compare it to the one on DeeDee's envelope.

THE COLOR IS EXACTLY THE SAME.

I'm trying to decide whether to inform Principal Jones or go directly to the Supreme Court when I hear humming in the hallway just outside the classroom. I recognize the tune. It sounds like the national anthem of a country where happiness is not allowed.

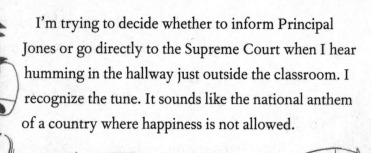

More important, it is the *exact same song* Mrs. Bunyan used to hum to herself when she thought no one was listening!

While my heart and my stomach have a wrestling match, I leap across the room and into the closet just as the door to the classroom swings open.

The lights flip on, and the humming gets louder as Mr. Shine comes up to the front of the room and walks toward the closet.

I suddenly understand how statues must feel. I can't move and can't speak and have no idea what I would do or say if I could.

Mr. Shine opens the closet, hangs up his coat, and shuts the door again, all without noticing the me-sized human being huddled in the corner.

WHEW.

I slowly remember how to breathe as the rest of the class files in, chattering about kickball and superheroes and, of course, the Squiggler.

Once everyone is settled, Mr. Shine begins the lesson. The same way he always does.

Who knows where limestone comes from?

No one speaks. Because we have no idea. *Because he hasn't told us yet!*

What do you think, Bob?

The ground?

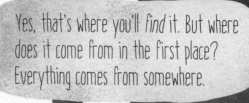

Yes, that's where you'll *find* it. But where does it come from in the first place? Everything comes from somewhere.

Just then, my leg starts to itch, and when I bend down to give it a good scratch, my foot bumps into . . .

a box of . . .

ENVELOPES!

(WHITE!) ← → (MEDIUM-ISH!)

The exact same color and size as the envelope that Roy's letter was in!

ROY

Teachers teach. Which means they need books and chalk and paper. I try to think of EVEN ONE REASON why Mr. Shine would need a box of envelopes.

Who needs envelopes?

Squigglers!

I close my eyes and tap my toes and try to *think*. In addition to having a purple marker and a suspicious box of envelopes,

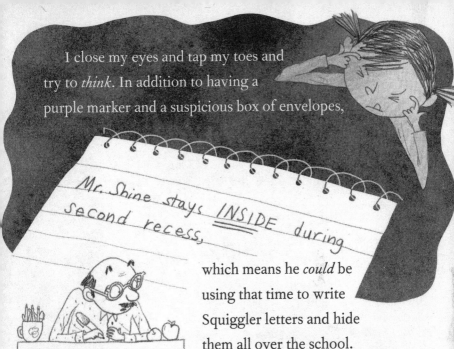

Mr. Shine stays <u>INSIDE</u> during second recess,

which means he *could* be using that time to write Squiggler letters and hide them all over the school.

But then there's Tracy Dublinger, who I know for a fact was inside during *first* recess and has purple smudges all over her *guilty right hand*.

Either one of them could be the Squiggler.

BUT WHO?

I don't know for sure. And until I know for sure, I cannot tell Principal Jones.

EVIDENCE, PLEASE.

My goodness! You're right. Has anyone seen Moxie?

I know I saw her at recess.

It's the voice of history's most lovable traitor, Emily Estevez, who is probably, at this moment, plotting my tragic downfall in the kindest way possible.

I saw her come back *inside*,

says Tracy.

A few minutes *before* recess ended.

Well, that's strange,

says Mr. Shine.

Do you have any idea why she might have done that?

It sort of looked like she might have been up to no good.

Now Tammy is speaking. I know because her voice is *ever so slightly* less irritating than Tracy's. I can almost picture them giving each other an evil-twin

I don't think that's true, says Emily.

I agree with Tammy, says Tracy.

There was a worrisome gleam in Moxie's eye. You'd better let Principal Jones know we might all be in danger.

Things are spiraling out of control. If I wait any longer, Tracy Dublinger is going to blame me for starting the REVOLUTIONARY WAR.

I have no choice. I must take action.

And so I open the door, walk confidently out of the closet, smile at Mr. Shine, and say as cheerfully as I can,

Well, gosh, I guess that wasn't the bathroom after all.

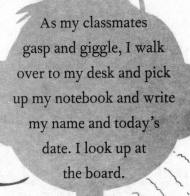

As my classmates gasp and giggle, I walk over to my desk and pick up my notebook and write my name and today's date. I look up at the board.

My **HEART** is pounding so loudly I can barely hear myself speak as I say,

Am I correct that we are discussing limestone?

"You are correct," says Mr. Shine. I can't tell whether he is reconsidering his Owl Point policy or whether he thinks I might actually have been looking for the bathroom. But he doesn't seem mad and doesn't seem fooled. Maybe he suspects I've found his envelopes and purple marker. But if he's worried, he doesn't show it. The rest of the class is waiting for me to get sent to see Principal Jones, but Mr. Shine just continues with the lesson.

"Tracy, you were right about how limestone is formed—from little pieces of

SEDIMENT.

That's why it's called

SEDIMENTARY

rock. Who knows the other basic kinds of rocks?"

Hank Harwood, who never, ever—and I mean *never*—raises his hand, raises his hand.

NEVER

EVER

Volcano rocks?

Very close, Hank. Rocks that form when magma cools are called *igneous* rocks.

 Mr. Shine smiles and Hank smiles back.

Somehow, in Mr. Shine's class, it's okay to raise your hand, because you're pretty sure he's not going to bite it off if you get the answer wrong.

I'm stuck between suspecting
Mr. Shine of darkest crimes and
feeling thankful that he didn't get
mad at me for the closet caper.

I just don't know what to think. I'm full of feelings
and theories and hunches, but what I need is some rock-solid
evidence. Which means it's time to roll up my sleeves and
do what Annabelle would.

Which is find clues.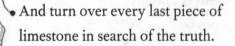

And question suspects.

And turn over every last piece of
limestone in search of the truth.

I fight the temptation to glance over at
Emily until I can't fight it anymore. She is
staring at her notebook. Looking sad and
lonely and a little bit lost.

Good, I tell myself, trying
my hardest to believe it.

CHAPTER 11: DEAR JOHN

The next day at recess, our lines are even longer. A bunch *more* kids have been Squiggled. Suddenly, I have more cases than I can handle, which means a big stack of letters and envelopes to carefully examine for patterns and clues.

Almost every letter has a different kind of handwriting, which means the Squiggler is obviously a hardened criminal.

In Volume 16:

John Hancockamamie,

a street musician who goes by

JENNY STARZ XVI

(HER ACTUAL NAME IS GERTRUDE DULL)

sends herself 50,000 pieces of fake fan mail, using different handwriting for each, in order to convince a big-time Nashville label to sign her to a record deal.

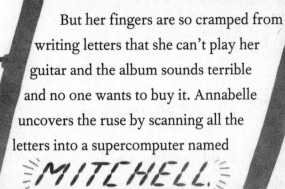

But her fingers are so cramped from writing letters that she can't play her guitar and the album sounds terrible and no one wants to buy it. Annabelle uncovers the ruse by scanning all the letters into a supercomputer named

MITCHELL.

But I do not have a supercomputer.
And I don't have 50,000 fans. Yet.

A few of the envelopes are the white rectangular kind I found in Mr. Shine's closet, but there are lots of colors and shapes. Either Mr. Shine has a bunch of *other* kinds of envelopes hidden somewhere else, or he actually *isn't* the Squiggler.

The answers
must be buried
somewhere in the mountain
of evidence. But try as I might, I
can't figure out what to make of it.

I could beat a cheetah in a footrace.

I could intimidate the empress of the mountain gorillas.

But careful observing and drawing conclusions is what sidekicks are for.

I know someone who is very, very good at this sort of thing, but at the moment, he's extremely busy sticking a fork in my **HEART**.

It occurs to me that I might be able to find someone *else* to handle this sort of unpleasant work. I look around for possible candidates and finally settle on lost-ball John, who

☑ is very good at math (attentive to details)

☑ sometimes counts blades of grass during recess (extremely patient)

☑ and is the owner of the second Squiggler letter (the critical piece of evidence!).

Perhaps it holds the to the entire mystery.

I will talk to John at lunchtime.
For now, I have another important
task. I have been keeping one eye on
Tracy Dublinger, who, as usual, has
been playing tetherball with Tammy.

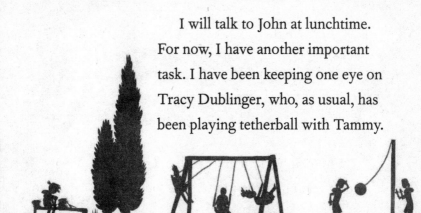

About halfway through recess, Tracy says something to
Tammy and heads for the doors to the school. Strangely, she
walks right past the teachers and slips inside without any of
them saying a word!

This is my chance to find out what Tracy is
up to! And so I take a deep breath and try to look
confident and walk right past the teachers, too.
Amazingly, incredibly, it works!

Almost.

Where are you going, Moxie?

It's Mr. Shine.

I . . . just have to go to the bathroom.

That's fine. But please ask first next time.

I'm tempted to point out that Tracy
didn't ask, but I don't have time for chitchat.

Absolutely,

I say.

I must have smog in my noggin.

Mr. Shine gives me a huge smile.

You must!

I smile, too. I just can't help myself. In
spite of my suspicions and the growing heap
of evidence, Mr. Shine just *seems* like a kind,
friendly person. It's *so hard* to not like him.
Which is why I need to follow my *other*
suspect. To find out for sure that she, and not
Mr. Shine, is the Squiggler in question.

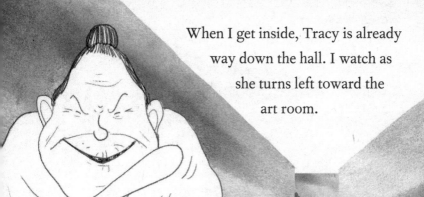

When I get inside, Tracy is already way down the hall. I watch as she turns left toward the art room.

Again, I am baffled by how she was able to walk past the front office without being seen and captured and bound and gagged and eaten alive by Mrs. Breath.

I decide not to risk it and instead take the long way around, darting quietly past the sixth-grade classroom and music room and cafeteria until I reach the far back corner where the art room is.

I peek through the door. Tracy is there, sitting at a table with her back to me. She is hunched over and her arm is moving as if she's writing something.

Without warning,
I sneeze so loud my ears ring.
It happens sometimes.

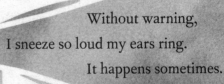

Tracy whips her
head around, and for
just a fraction of a
second, I see her
holding . . . a
purple marker!

Before she can see me seeing her, I duck my head and
sprint back down the hallway and into the sunshine.

Are you okay?

asks Mr. Shine, probably
wondering why I'm so out of breath.

I am in an excellent mood,   I say.

Because it's true. I may not have enough evidence
to throw Tracy in jail—not yet—but she certainly seemed
to be Squiggling.

Now I just need to build an **IRON&CLAD** case.

Which is where my new "partner" comes in.

I wait for John by the cafeteria door.

"Hello, John," I say, backing him slowly toward a table in the far corner.

"Don't hurt me," he says.

"I'm not going to hurt you John," I say. "I just want to chat."

"Milton said I wasn't supposed to talk to you."

"Of course. But that was *before*."

"Before what?"

"Before . . . before I offered you a *job*."

A *job?*

John, I like how you think! The answer is yes. Welcome to the agency. Your first assignment is telling me everything you know about Milton's case.

191

Milton said that stuff was top secret.

That was when you were his *client*, John. Now you are my *partner*. It is essential that you tell your partner EVERYTHING related to our cases. Our case is not about *your* letter. It's about *Emily's* letter. But in order to figure out who sent *Emily's* letter, we need to know as much as possible about the letter sent to *John Potter*.

I'm John Potter.

John Potter is our *client*. You're my *partner*. The letter is the *evidence*. Isn't it essential that we, the detectives, examine the critical piece of *evidence*?

192

John looks like he just stepped off an especially twisty roller coaster. "I guess so," he says, reaching into his pocket and pulling out an envelope with no return address, no stamp, and a purple squiggle.

> ♥ ♥ ♥ ♥ ♥ ♥ ♥ ♥
> Dear John,
> I want you to know how much I appreciate you. You are the best. You are so kind and so friendly. I really like you. Always remember that you are great. Remember not to let anyone take advantage of you.
> — The person you'd least expect

> The words of John's letter make me feel ever so slightly guilty about the current situation.

But not enough to lose sight of the problem at hand. I need John, and John needs my protection from the Squiggler.

I slide John's letter into my pocket, and when he starts to protest, I take his hand, look him in the eye, and speak in a calm and steady voice.

"Have a seat."

"I was about to get my lunch."

"No lunch today, John."

"But I'm so hungry."

"*There is no time for hunger!*
This is your big opportunity to

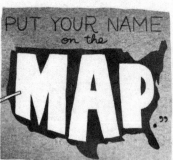

PUT YOUR NAME on the MAP."

"I think I'd lose an Owl Point if I wrote on the map."

"Forget the map!" I say, handing John my stack of letters. "Study these and tell me what you find. I want to see *patterns*, John. I want to see *irregularities*. I want to know *everything* you can tell me about the Squiggler. How she thinks! What she wants! What type of speedboat she uses to rob tugboats on the South China Sea!"

"What do speedboats—?"

"I have *full confidence* in you, John. Now, please begin. We don't have a moment to spare."

ONE, TWO, THREE... ...THIRTY-TWO... ...SIXTY-SIX... TWELVE, ELEVEN... ...QUINCE, CATORCE... UNO!

I know John needs time to think, so I eat my sandwich slowly. I pace back and forth. I count backward from 50 and then backward from 100. Then backward from 50 in Spanish. I keep waiting for John to leap up and say AHA! or EUREKA!! or SQUIGGLER, I RENOUNCE THEE! but instead he keeps on sighing like a weary walrus.

Time's up, John. What can you tell me about the Squiggler?

—UM...

WELL...

John says a few *um*s and then a few *well*s. Probably because he has reached incredibly exciting conclusions and wants to build up to them gradually.

I'm pretty sure the Squiggler . . .

I consider
telling John that
I'm pretty sure the
Squiggler is also a

HUMAN BEING from **PLANET EARTH**

but he looks fragile, and I am holding out hope that he might
still say something useful.

"Thank you, John. What else?"

"The Squiggler . . . likes to make squiggles?"

My hope is fading fast.

"Excuse me, John. But have you come to any *useful*
conclusions?"

John blinks.

"Do you have any theories,
however flawed or implausible?"

John gulps.

DO I NEED TO
FEED YOU TO THE
ALLIGATOR, JOHN?

Of course there is no alligator. But John doesn't know that.

He looks at me with wild eyes.

"I *do* have a theory . . . that the Squiggler might be . . . Tracy Dublinger."

Suddenly, John has said something *extremely* interesting.

"Go on."

"Tracy goes to Tiddlywhump."

By that logic, *I* could be the Squiggler, John. By that logic, *you* could be the Squiggler.

"There's something else."

"Yes?"

"Tracy has a . . . purple marker." John gestures with his eyes to a table on the other side of the cafeteria.

I look. And yes! Tracy Dublinger is, at that very moment, writing on something with a . . . purple marker *out in front of everyone*!

HOW CAN SHE BE SO CARELESS? HOW CAN SHE BE SO BOLD?!

Tracy sees me staring at her and quickly covers up whatever she is writing with her tray.

What else, John? What do you see in the data? What is her *motive*, John? Do you have any **IRONCLAD** proof?

It's more of a hunch.

But suddenly I have *enormous* confidence in John and his hunches.

 Both of us came to the same conclusion independently. Which has to mean something.

Tracy has a proven record of wickedness.

 She is exactly the kind of person who would deliberately send notes that seemed nice but were actually part of a dark scheme to . . . to . . . ?

To get rid of Emily and . . . anyone else who . . . who . . . ? Who . . . might be her competition for the Wise Owl Award, which is given twice a year to the student with the *very best grades*!

Tracy loves winning the Wise Owl Award as much as Santa Claus loves taking a long, luxurious nap the day after Christmas. She would stop at nothing to squash the competition!

And suddenly, we have

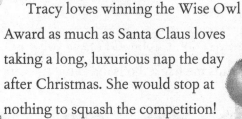

I make a mental note to figure out whether the students getting Squiggled are also the ones with the very best grades.

Emily *does* get excellent grades!

+ And she *did* get a letter.

+ I *do not* have the very best grades.

+ And I *have not* gotten a letter.

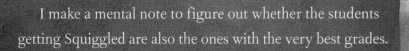

= (It's all starting to add up.

"The question, John, is how we *prove* it was Tracy. Do you have any ideas?"

"Um . . ."

"Of course you don't, John. Of *course* you don't."

But then it hits me like a thousand cannons firing at the very same time.

  "We need Milton's lie detector!"

"What for?"

 "All we have to do is put the baseball cap on Tracy's head and make her hold the tennis ball and ask her point-blank if she's the Squiggler. While Principal Jones and the FBI take notes and get the handcuffs ready. *It's the perfect plan!*"

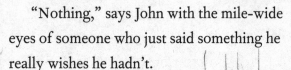

"But the lie detector doesn't actually work."

"What?" I say. Because it sounds like John just said that the lie detector doesn't work.

"Nothing," says John with the mile-wide eyes of someone who just said something he really wishes he hadn't.

"Oh, you sure said something, John."

John is shaking his head back and forth so hard I'm afraid it's going to fall off.

I stand over John. I get up on my tippy-toes. I give him Annabelle's signature

DEEP ARCTIC STARE.

The time has come to freeze the truth right out of him.

Is Milton's lie detector fake, John?

Let's just say it needs some work.

I lower the Stare to Absolute Zero.

Your stare! It's *unbearable!*

It will all be over soon, John. Tell me about the lie detector.

Mostly it just flashes and beeps.

I knew it!

I release John from the stare. I have the information I need.

"I figured you knew," says John. "I thought you and Milton were *partners*."

"We *were*," I say. "The same way Martha Washington was once a first lady."

"I thought you said partners tell each other everything."

"They do," I say. "Or at least, they *should*. But to be honest, John, I was never sure about the whole partner thing in the first place. I should have listened to my

"If you didn't want to be Milton's partner, why did you sign the agency agreement?"

"Here's the thing, John. I'm a sucker for a nice-looking document. It had an attractive blue border and a shiny gold seal. It was utterly irresistible."

John's eyes light up. "That's classic Danny Doogood."

At the mention of Danny, I get a sour taste in my mouth. "What do you mean?"

"At the end of Book 2, Danny makes a *fancy-looking DOCUMENT* with a blue border and tells Rex it's a prize Rex can win if he goes an entire day without belching at school. At first, Rex isn't interested because he really likes belching, but when Danny adds the gold seal and says the prize is from the president, Rex decides to try really hard."

My blood is **BOILING.**

Not only did Milton lie about the lie detector, but he also fooled me into signing the document with a trick he learned from *Danny Doogood*!

THIS WILL NOT DO!!

John, this has been extremely helpful. But I'm afraid this partnership is officially over.

↶ John is stuck somewhere between ↷

DEEPLY DISAPPOINTED & COMPLETELY RELIEVED.

I flip him a quarter.

Here you go.

John hasn't worked a full day, but I'm too mad to make change. I glance across the lunchroom at Milton, who is using a ruler to make some sort of diagram.

I consider going over and doing my best impression of Rex, but there isn't time before the end of lunch to unleash all the lions ROARING inside me.

Finally, second recess comes.

On one hand, I want to devour Milton like a praying mantis devours her unsuspecting mate. On the other hand, he is technically my brother, and I know Mom would be disappointed if he were not available for hugging when she gets home from Africa.

PLAY NICE, SWEETIE!

But Milton crossed a line, and I have to speak my mind. I march over to his bench and glare at him with the fury of a thousand leaping dragons. He glares back with the fury of a hundred sleepy oysters.

I do not appreciate being lied to!

What are you talking about?

"The lie detector! It doesn't actually work, does it?"
Milton looks proud. "It never did."

"And once you used the

to make sure I *hadn't* read

you used Danny's irresistible
document trick to fool *me* into

didn't you?"

"I did," says Milton. He doesn't seem even sort of sorry,
which makes me even madder.

"Danny fools Rex in order to help *Rex*. You fooled me to
help *yourself*!"

Milton makes a face like someone just pointed out he's
not wearing pants. Before I can stop myself, I say
the single most hurtful thing I can think of.

You, Milton McCoy, are no Danny Doogood!

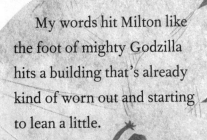

My words hit Milton like
the foot of mighty Godzilla
hits a building that's already
kind of worn out and starting
to lean a little.

He sputters and stammers and spits before saying,

Well, you're no Annabelle Adams.

His words make no sense, as if he's speaking Dutch.

Nou, je bent een kippen poep.

What do you mean?

I saw you picking on John. Annabelle would never
take advantage of a pigeon-toed first grader.

And of course she wouldn't, and of course *I* wouldn't, either.

207

"I wasn't *taking advantage* of John. He's my *partner!*"

I glance around the playground for John. I need to let him know that

says Milton.

Milton says the word *interesting* the way you might squash a mosquito that just landed on your arm.

It's then I notice that Milton has a new sign, written by hand on a piece of notebook paper and taped to a ruler that's jammed into the ground. Even though it's small and undignified and hard to read, it feels bigger than the side of a warehouse.

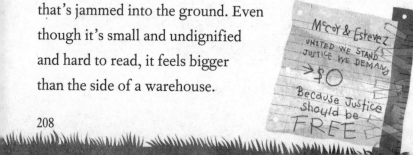

I have accepted that my partner has abandoned me.

I grudgingly admit that my agency is in ruins.

I can just barely live with the fact that my best friend has betrayed me.

But for Milton and Emily to be partners *and* have an agency that uses *our* motto *and* works for *free*!! It's every bad thing in the world wrapped up in one. Like a bowl of marshmallow soup at a Dublinger birthday party.

And just so you know,

says Milton, standing on his toes to look as tall as he can,

Emily and I are going to solve this mystery. *We* are going to unmask the Squiggler. And *you* are going to see what I'm capable of.

I feel flat as a shadow. I can't tell whether I'm mad or sad or sorry or some combination of all three.

Mostly I'm having trouble feeling much of anything.

I walk away in a foggy daze, back to my bench, where a handful of kids are waiting for me to solve their problems. I feel like telling them to go away, that I have too many problems of my own to deal with today.

But that's not what Annabelle would do.

And so I sit on my bench and take a deep breath and try to pretend that everything is right in the world.

A fifth grader named Amanda is first in line.

What seems to be the problem?

I just got this mysterious letter.

Let me have a look.

That night after
dinner, we do not gather
in the living room for FRIDAY
Family FUN
GAME NIGHT with Dad.

Milton goes straight to his room, and I go straight to mine.

I burrow under my blankets and take out my flashlight
and read the second and third Danny Doogood books,
from cover to cover
without stopping.

At first, I am hopeful.
Book 2 begins with Danny getting
bitten by a snake! But as it turns out, it was just
a regular old non-poisonous snake, and Danny learns a
valuable lesson about always wearing boots when walking in
tall grass. Everything just gets even more boring from there.

At one point, for example, Danny has to choose between

attending his cousin Flora's viola recital **AND** visiting his sick friend Richard in the hospital.

Danny doesn't want to disappoint Flora. But he also doesn't want Richard to think he doesn't care.

Danny is ✂ *torn!*

After spending two heart-wrenching hours staring in the mirror, asking

Who are you, Danny, and what do you believe in?

Danny calls Flora and explains that even though he really wants to hear her sonata in C minor, he's pretty sure Richard needs his company more. Flora is mildly disappointed but tells Danny she totally understands and will invite him to her next recital instead.

Danny is relieved and writes in his journal,

Never try to be two places at once. IT'S IMPOSSIBLE.

Which, I hate to admit, is not the worst advice I've ever heard.

Danny might be a rule-following goody two-shoes of a brown-nosing suck-up, but beneath it all, he's just a kid who's marching through his complicated life and trying to do the right thing.

Just like Annabelle does. Just like I do. Every single minute of my life.

CHAPTER 12: THE TRULY HORRIBLE MUFFIN

It rains all weekend, which is fine with me, because all I want to do is reread Annabelle. Diving into her adventures is like drinking a milk shake when you have a sore throat.

At recess on Monday, there is no kickball game. There are more mysterious letters than anyone can count. Pretty much everyone is standing in line. Pretty much everyone has gotten a letter. Everyone but me, that is.

I continue to elude the Squiggler's awful clutches.

214

If Tracy is following Fungo's

 *Death by Envelope* plan (and I have no reason to believe that she isn't), as soon as everyone with really good grades has a letter, she'll unleash the *next* phase of her diabolical scheme. *But what will it be?* Surely not building a shoe factory. *Then what?* Activating poisonous ink that will make her victims forget how to spell? Unleashing subliminal messages that will transform them into an army of brainwashed zombie henchmen who are really bad at math?

4×8=9

$\frac{7}{+2}$ = 72

WHUT?

$4\overline{)40}$ = 17

orinj

1+1= 68

BRAINZZ!

I glance over at Milton's bench. There is Emily, my bighearted, good-graded former best friend. Even though we are distant as opposite sides of the ocean, I will do anything to protect her.

As we sit there answering Mr. Shine's crazy questions and not really learning anything, I keep an eye on Tracy. If I am going to expose her as the Squiggler, I'll need to catch her off guard. I think and I think.

At lunch, I snarf my sandwich and sneak down to the art room, where I borrow some paper and a purple marker and do what must be done.

Back in class, Mr. Shine is standing at the blackboard, writing multiplication problems and calling us up one at a time to solve them. Don't get me wrong. I think math is fascinating and useful and even kind of fun, but watching someone else do math is about as exciting as watching an earthworm take a nap.

Which is why it's the perfect time to provide a little pleasant diversion.

I open my binder as dramatically as possible.

Oh my goodness! I whisper, lassoing my classmates with my eyes as I pull out the envelope I *just happen* to find tucked into the pocket.

A letter? For me?

I pause, letting everyone get a good, long look before I continue.

There's no stamp! But there is a purple squiggle!

The entire class is looking now. Fortunately, Mr. Shine is so busy helping poor George Wallaby remember how to carry the one that he doesn't seem to notice.

And so I read the letter, whispering aloud to myself so the other kids can hear all the thoughtful, amazing, wonderful things the Squiggler has to say about me.

Moxie,

I want you to know how much I appreciate you.

Your the world's best detective and your only in fourth grade which is amazing and our school is lucky to have you keeping us safe from contstant threats and peril and if anyone doubts you remember there just jealous.

— The person you'd least expect

Your the best!

oxie!

"Oh my *gosh*! This is so *nice*! I don't *deserve* such kind words!"

I glance around the room. Everyone is excited. As they should be. The Squiggler has struck again!

I feel Tracy's eyes on my skin like an awful burning rash. I allow myself the tiniest glance in her direction. But I can't read her expression. Is it the scowl of an enraged Squiggler wondering how *I* got one of her letters? Or is it the look of a jealous classmate who wishes it were *her* name on the envelope?

I am sitting there in the crossfire of Dublinger disapproval and trying to piece things together when Mr. Shine looks at me and smiles.

> Moxie, if you're done reading your top secret letter, would you please come up to the board and do some math with me?

The class laughs. Any other teacher would have taken the letter away, along with an Owl Point or two.

As I slip my letter back into my binder and walk toward the board, I hear Milton making logical arguments in my head.

It's so *unlikely* that Mr. Shine kidnapped Mrs. Bunyan. It's probably just a *coincidence* that he has the same pink hat and talks about noggins filled with smog. And the fact that he and Mrs. Bunyan *both* whistle the same strange song doesn't prove *anything*.

= unlikely

= coincidence

= coincidence

= proves NOTHING

As for the possibility that Mr. Shine could be the Squiggler, there are *plenty* of purple markers and envelopes in the world. It's *not at all* strange for a teacher to have them in his classroom. And *when would he have had the time* to write and deliver all those letters? I glance back at Tracy, who continues to pelt me with her

beady ▶ little ▶ eye ▶ missiles.

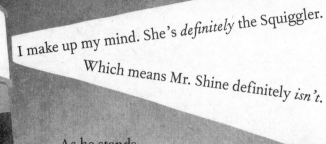

I make up my mind. She's *definitely* the Squiggler.

Which means Mr. Shine definitely *isn't*.

As he stands
there smiling like
a lighthouse guiding sailboats
through a dark and foggy night, I decide
Mr. Shine actually *is* the kind and cheerful,
bighearted, admittedly-odd-but-frankly-
quite-wonderful person that he seems to be.

But just a moment later, as I walk past his desk on my
way to the blackboard, I see something that makes my throat
seize and my heart pound and my skin grow cold. Something
that changes absolutely everything.

There, on the corner of Mr. Shine's desk, is a muffin I recognize. A large and lopsided bran muffin with yellow raisins and white-chocolate chips and rainbow sprinkles.

The muffin is nestled in a metallic green cupcake wrapper and is sitting on a pink plastic party plate.

But by far the strangest thing about the muffin is the tiny Swedish flag on a toothpick planted in the center.

It's a muffin that Mrs. Bunyan would bring to eat for lunch at least once a week.

The hat and the song and the smog in the noggin *could* just be remarkable coincidences. But this muffin is the very definition of weirdly one-of-a-kind. No other human being on this planet or any other planet would make such a muffin.

SET THE OVEN TO 450°, ALEXA!

Not only has Mr. Shine kidnapped Mrs. Bunyan, but *he's also forcing her to bake for him*!

I'm trying my hardest to multiply

26
× 39

but am completely distracted by the fact that I'm standing inches from *the worst kind of criminal*!

The numbers blur, the chalk shakes, and Mr. Shine tells me we'll try again later.

As I pass the horrible muffin on the way back to my desk, it might as well be screaming,

I have no idea what to do next, so I decide to read my letter again. Even though those kind words came out of my own head, I really need some kind of boost. I open my binder, but the letter isn't there. Which is impossible, because I definitely left it in the pocket.

That's when I hear snickering to my left.

Tracy Dublinger is holding my letter and shaking her head.

Look, Moxie, whoever sent this letter spelled the word *you're* wrong, just like you always do. *And* the word *they're*. What a coincidence! And *look*, there are some commas missing in the *exact same places* that *you* always forget to write commas.

Give me my letter, I say. I do not say it nicely.

I can't remember . . . Moxie . . . did you say this letter is TO you or FROM you?

Tracy is speaking not very quietly. Suddenly, everyone is paying 100% attention to us.

Give it back, I snarl.

In a minute, says Tracy.

There's something fishy going on, and I'm trying to get to the bottom of it.

GIVE IT BACK!

Tracy looks at me with smirking eyes, and I feel as naked as the day I was born.

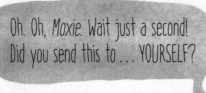

Oh. Oh, *Moxie*. Wait just a second!
Did you send this to . . . YOURSELF?

As she hands the letter back to me, Tracy makes a face I've never seen from her before. It turns out the only thing worse than being disliked by a Dublinger is being pitied by one.

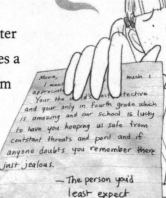

Moxie,
I want appreciat . . . much I
Your the . . . ld's best . . . tective
and your only in fourth grade which
is amazing and our school is lucky
to have you keeping us safe from
contstant threats and peril and if
anyone doubts you remember there
just jealous.

— The person you'd
least expect

The class gasps and giggles as Tracy gloats. I want to melt into a puddle so our custodian, Mr. Hammer, can mop me up and wring me out in the utility sink. I want to drain away into the pipes and escape to the distant sea.

I want to be anywhere but where I am.

I make the mistake of glancing at Emily just as she is glancing at me. We lock eyes for a sliver of a second, then both look away, not sure we can stand to face how we'd feel if we looked a second longer.

I need to get out of the room. Right now. Without raising my hand, I head for the door.

I need to go to the principal's office,

I say, not even waiting for my hall pass.

Mr. Shine doesn't try to stop me. Probably because he knows it would be impossible.

CHAPTER 13: LEARNING TO PADDLE

When I get to the front of the school, I do not stop for a pleasant chat with Mrs. Breath. I walk right into Principal Jones's office and sit down on her bench.

Moxie, this is inappropriate,

she says, but then she stops talking because I interrupt her.

I wouldn't have barged in if it weren't extremely—

But that's all I manage to get out before Principal Jones says,

It's all right, Moxie. It's going to be all right.

She hands me a tissue and then another tissue, and suddenly she's giving me a hug. This is entirely unprofessional, of course, and I do my best to pull myself together, but that turns out to be harder than usual.

"Why don't you tell me what's going on?"

"Mrs. Bunyan!"

"What about her?"

"She has been . . . kidnapped!"

"I'm afraid I don't understand."

EVIDENCE

hat

smog

muffin

I explain about the pink hat with the purple daisy. About "smog in my noggin" and Mr. Shine whistling Mrs. Bunyan's song. And then I take a deep breath and describe the horrible muffin, sparing no gruesome detail.

Principal Jones frowns, as if remembering an unpleasant dream.

I was once forced to eat one of those muffins.

"Before we see about rescuing Mrs. Bunyan, is there anything else that's bothering you?"

"What do you mean?"

"In my experience, you're usually concerned about more than one thing at a time."

"Well. Yes. The 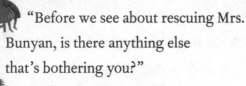 letters."

"Yes, I think they're rather nice."

I stand up and look Principal Jones in the eye.

"Excuse me, Principal Jones, but *they are not nice*! They are part of a diabolical plot to ensure the downfall of Emily Estevez and Tiddlywhump Elementary and maybe even the entire town!"

"The entire *town*?"

"Maybe even the entire *world*!"

"Oh my. And it sounds like you're having trouble figuring out who's sending them."

I want to tell her I know EXACTLY who's sending them, but I also know Principal Jones will want actual proof. And so far, all I have is purple ink and a suspect with a history of sneakiness.

"It's a very tricky case."

"I thought you and Milton were the best in the business."

"I might be working alone this time."

"Oh? Why is that?"

I go through a few more tissues and explain about the fake lie detector and the irresistibly beautiful document with the blue border and gold seal and how Milton pulled a classic Danny Doogood and how I consider his actions an unforgivable act of utmost TREACHERY.

FAKE!

IRRESISTIBLE!?

PURE GOLD!

MORE LIKE CLASSICALLY LAME!

Principal Jones takes down a framed certificate from her wall. It has a fancy blue border and a shiny gold seal.

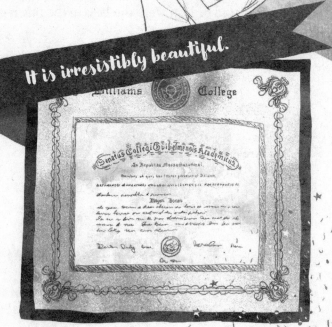

It is irresistibly beautiful.

Williams College

"What's *that*?"

"My college diploma. My mom once told me that if I worked very hard for a long time, I would get a magical piece of paper that would make incredible things happen in my life."

"Is it really magic?"

"Well. It's the reason I'm allowed to be a principal."

"That *is* an incredible thing."

"It certainly is. But you know what? I didn't know I wanted to be a principal way back then. And I really didn't want to do all the hard work. I just knew I wanted this piece of paper."

"So your mom tricked you?"

"Maybe. Mostly she just believed in me. Why do you think Milton tricked you?"

I sit there for a minute, admiring the diploma.

"Because he believes in me?"

"And?"

"Because he wanted to be my partner?"

"I think that's right. You want to know a secret?"

I am convinced this is the moment when Principal Jones is finally going to show me the lever that opens the trapdoor above the eel tank.

ABSoLUTELY, I say.

But as it turns out, she's talking about something else.

"This diploma is just an ordinary piece of paper. There's no magic in it. I could tear it up and I'd still be a principal. The actual magic is here," she says, pointing to her head.

I think about that.

"How long have you been trying to identify the Squiggler on your own?"

"A week."

"And when you worked with Milton to find Eddie, how long did it take?"

"About five hours."

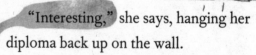

"Interesting," she says, hanging her diploma back up on the wall.

I'm just about to tell Principal Jones that Tracy Dublinger is without a doubt the Squiggler when I notice something on her desk. A stack of homemade posters drawn with . . . purple ink.

Principal Jones sees me staring. "Want to see?" she says, holding them up. "They're for the

SPRING CONCERT."

Those drawings are really good. Who did them?

Tracy. She's been volunteering as a Recess Helper for the past few weeks—spending the second half of first recess in the art room making these.

Tracy . . . *Dublinger?*

My mind is swirling around like furniture in a tornado.

235

"Yes. This is her way of letting me know how sorry she is about what happened with Eddie."

I say nothing. There is nothing to say.

"Tracy is a fine artist, don't you think?"

I hate to admit it, but she absolutely is. I wish I could draw even half as well. But any shred of evidence that she's also a fine Squiggler has just gone out the window.

The bell rings, which means it's time for second recess. I'm glad to be here with Principal Jones and not alone on my bench, watching

"Are you feeling any better?" asks Principal Jones.

I seem to be done with the tissues, so I hand her the box.

"I am."

"Good. Now let's see what we can do about that *other* problem."

"Mrs. Bunyan?"

Principal Jones gives me a dignified nod and pushes a button on her phone. Mr. Shine's voice comes through her speaker.

Yes?

Paul, could you come to my office for a minute?

Sure.

It takes me a second to realize that Paul and Mr. Shine are the same person.

Principal Jones moves papers around on her desk while I sit there in a PUDDLE OF DREAD. I've already told her that Mr. Shine is a dastardly kidnapper, but she doesn't seem the least concerned.

I look around her office for something I can use to defend myself.

There is a stapler on her desk.

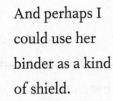

And perhaps I could use her binder as a kind of shield.

237

I'm contemplating various escape routes when the door opens. And there he is, Mr. Paul Shine, professional kidnapper.

"Hello," he says with his endless smile.

Principal Jones clears her throat. "Paul, as it turns out, Moxie has been missing Mrs. Bunyan and wonders if you might be able to tell us how she's doing."

"Oh? That's very sweet of you, Moxie. Let's see . . . right about now she's probably"—Mr. Shine looks at his watch—"sitting in my living room, watching

I KNEW IT!

Mr. Shine is holding Mrs. Bunyan hostage at his house! But . . . why is he admitting it? And why is Principal Jones so calm?

"But . . . why is she at your house?"

"She's been living with me for a few years now. Ever since my dad died, I've been taking care of her and . . . she's been taking care of me."

And all the  that have been rattling around in my head suddenly slide into place.

Mr. Shine knows Mrs. Bunyan's song because he grew up listening to her hum it.

He says *smog in my noggin* because he grew up listening to her say it.

He eats horrible muffins because Mrs. Bunyan has been feeding them to him for so long he doesn't know any better.

Mr. Shine has a pink knit hat with a purple daisy on the side because Mrs. Bunyan knit it for him.

And he wears it even though it's itchy and awful-looking because he loves her.

Mrs. Bunyan hasn't been kidnapped. Mrs. Bunyan gets to sit around relaxing and watching TV while her son asks us questions all day long.

Mrs. Bunyan is happy as a clam. Because she is Mr. Shine's mom!

"Thanks," I say. "I'm really glad to hear that."

Principal Jones gives me a wink.

"Should I tell her you said hello?" asks Mr. Shine.

"Absolutely," I say, though I wouldn't be surprised if Mrs. Bunyan doesn't quite believe him when she hears it was from me.

SHE SAID WHAT ?!

"Moxie and I were just finishing our conversation," says Principal Jones.

"I'm heading back to the classroom," says Mr. Shine. "Want to come with me?"

"Sure," I say. I'll do anything to avoid recess.

I feel like I need to start from scratch with Mr. Shine. Now that I know he's not a kidnapper, I could see the possibility of us being rather good friends . . . as long as he's definitely *not* the SQUIGGLER.

May I ask you a *serious* question?

Absolutely.

Mr. Shine doesn't seem nervous the way some grownups do when you tell them you're going to get serious.

Are you . . . the Squiggler?

Who is the Squiggler?

I wonder for a second what rock Mr. Shine has been living under.

The Squiggler is the dark-hearted fiend who has been leaving anonymous letters all over the school, creating havoc and uncertainty.

Mr. Shine looks unconvinced.

And also . . .

happiness?

I have to admit, the Squiggler has been creating some happiness in addition to the havoc.

And also . . .

goodwill?

I have to admit that people have been pretty nice to one another lately.

We get back to the classroom, and I have a seat while Mr. Shine erases the board.

I want to tell him that the goodwill is just a prelude to the darkness to come, the way scary movies start with a baby deer munching grass in a peaceful meadow . . .

. . . before alien spaceships appear and turn the forest into a pile of soot and the baby deer into a mutant cyborg with lasers in its hooves.

But before I can explain this, Mr. Shine stops what he's doing and looks me straight in the eye.

Why are you trying to figure out who's sending these letters?

Because everybody wants to know. Because the other kids are counting on me. Because we might be in terrible danger.

Because . . .

And there I pause. Because he is so easy to talk to, I consider telling Mr. Shine every miserable detail of my truly awful week. I'm just not sure where to start. But Mr. Shine looks at me as if he already knows everything I'm trying to say.

Have you ever gone canoeing?

Once, on a camping trip. It was hard.

It *is* hard. You have to really be on the same page with someone to canoe with them.

Every summer, my brother and I go camping together. I like to camp on one side of the lake and he likes to camp on the other side. One day, we were out canoeing in the middle of the lake and it looked like it was going to rain.

He started paddling toward his side, and I started paddling toward mine.

What do you think happened?

"You didn't go anywhere."

"The canoe didn't move at all. And so we got rained on."

"Why didn't you just pick one side or the other?"

"Because we both thought we were right. Neither one of us would budge."

"Even when it started raining?"

"Yep, we just kept paddling in opposite directions for hours."

"But that's ridiculous. Why didn't one of you just—"

But I stop myself.
Because I know the answer.
Mr. Shine gives me a smile.

I don't know whether it's
Milton in the canoe with me

or maybe Emily

or possibly both,

but suddenly I'm really
tired of getting rained on.

I look at the clock. I have enough time.

"Do you mind if I go outside for the rest of recess?"

"I think you should," says Mr. Shine. "It's a beautiful day for a paddle."

CHAPTER 14: MISSING PERSONS

I rush outside. There they are on the far bench. On the other side of the lake. Milton and Emily. Emily and Milton. Two of the most important people in my life, who are, at the moment, not in my life at all.

 When I get to the bench, Milton slams his notebook shut and looks at me like a vampire looks at the sunrise. Emily stares down at her knees, as if her nose weighed 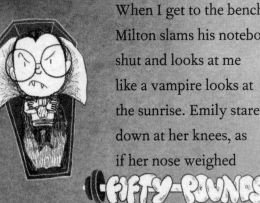 **FIFTY-POUNDS.**

It's clear I'm not welcome. But I dig deep and put on my best Mr. Shine—inspired smile.

Hello, Milton,

I say.

Hello, Emily. You are just the two people I wanted to see.

I have nothing to say to you, says Milton.

I understand that. And I wouldn't bother you if it weren't extremely important. But I have a serious problem. And I want to hire the two of you to solve it.

Our caseload is full.

Wait a second, says Emily.

What about bylaw #4, "Milton must discuss with Emily before accepting or declining any cases"? I'd like to hear what Moxie has to say.

Milton looks like a puppy that's being lifted by the scruff of its neck and really wants to get its paws back on the floor.

Ah yes, bylaw #4. You make a good point, *partner*. Perhaps we do have time for one more case. But we demand payment up front.

I glance over at the sign. "I thought justice should be free." "There are exceptions to every rule," says Milton, giving me a fierce look.

"Of course," I say, pulling out a

DOLLAR

and placing it in Milton's open palm.

As he puts it in his pocket
and hands two quarters to
Emily, he looks at me as if to say,

SEE HOW EASY THAT WAS?

Milton climbs up on the bench. Which means we're
standing pretty much eye-to-eye.

"Now, what seems to be the *problem*?" he asks.

"It's very serious,
actually. I'm here to report a

MISSING ? PERSON.

In fact, there are

→TWO← PEOPLE ? ? MISSING."

"When was the last time you saw the *first* missing person?"

"Tuesday afternoon. He disappeared off the edge of a
slippery roof." Milton looks up from his notebook.

"What happened?"

"Well . . . I might have called him *gnomish*."

WHAT'S WRONG WITH GNOMISH?

"It sounds like he had a pretty good reason to disappear."

"I can't argue with that. But a lot has changed since then. There's so much I'd like to tell him . . . *if* he were here."

"What would you say to . . . what was his name again?"

"Let's just call him my former *partner*."

"What would you say to your former partner? *If* he were here."

"Well . . . *if* he were here, I'd say I'm really sorry I broke four bylaws and that I didn't mean to be a bossy jerk and that I've collected lots of evidence but really need his great big brain to help me figure out what it all means."

Milton's scowl has softened a bit, but not entirely, which is okay because I'm not quite done.

"I'd also tell him that even though it was pretty sneaky to build a fake lie detector and trick me into signing an irresistible document, I'm pretty sure he did it because he believes in me. And because he believes in *us*."

Milton looks at me as if I've told most of a joke and he's waiting for the punch line.

"*Finally*, I'd want to tell him that if he'd give me a second chance, I really, really want to be his partner again. Because, let's face it, it's pretty much impossible to stand united all by yourself."

Milton looks like he wants to say something but can't quite get his mouth to open.

I look at him like I've been paddling in his
direction for a while now and
feel like it's his turn
to pick up an
oar.

We blink at each other.

This boat is going nowhere.

I hear Emily clear her throat.

What about the *other* missing person?

she asks.

Her eyes are full of hope.

First off, she's the greatest and the best, from her perfect smile to her great big heart. She's good, she's kind, she's patient . . . and extremely loyal.

What happened to her?

It's hard to admit. But I pushed her away.

Why?

Because I was jealous. And mad. And acting like a big, dumb baby.

Emily looks at me like the first rays of sun coming over the mountains really early in the morning.

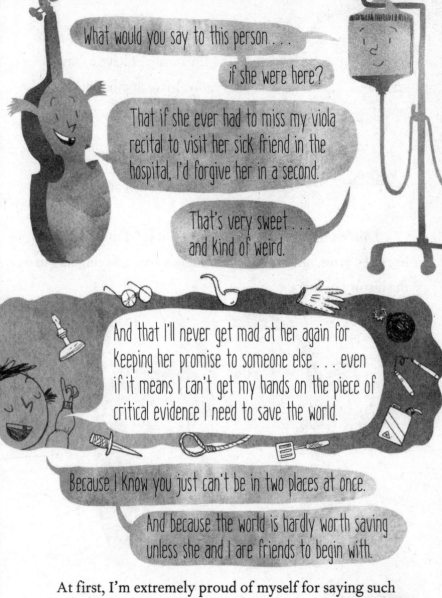

At first, I'm extremely proud of myself for saying such wise things, but then I have an awful moment and realize I learned them from awful Danny Doogood.

MAN, I'M GOOD!

Emily is smiling now, so I finish what I have to say. "Finally, I would point out that I miss her more than anything. That I'm so, so, so, so sorry. That she is—I mean *was*—my very best friend in the whole wide world."

"Don't worry," says Emily. "She still is." I tumble into her open arms, and we have the single most satisfying hug in the history of hugs.

Now Milton clears *his* throat.

A-HEM.

I believe I *have* seen your missing partner.

You *have?*

I have. And while he appreciates your apology and might be willing to work with you again, he regrets to inform you that he *already has* an excellent partner.

About that. I think I'm ready to retire. I'm just not cut out to be a detective.

Milton looks wounded. "This is unexpected."

I'm sorry, but questioning suspects gives me a jittery stomach. I'm going to let you guys get down to business.

Emily gives me
a warm smile
and then walks off.

Once she's safely out of earshot, I turn to Milton and say, "I *really* missed you. John couldn't puzzle his way out of a box full of baby chicks."

"I've missed you, too," he says. "Emily is way too nice to do the dirty work."

"What do you mean?"

"She didn't know how to persuade our clients to let us keep their letters, so I couldn't take a close look at them. And when people didn't want to reveal important information, she didn't know how to get them to talk."

She wasn't, you know . . .

you.

Hearing this is like getting an extra scoop of ice cream on my apple cobbler.

I put my hand on Milton's shoulder and get down to business. "I have a big  that need careful analysis."

His eyes light up. "And I have several theories, but not enough **DATA** to make sense of them."

"Should we give this partnership another try?"

Milton thinks. I can see the spark plugs firing behind his eyeballs.

Yes . . . BUT.

But what?

You have to actually follow the bylaws this time. *All of them.* Even the twice-daily compliments.

Okay. On one condition.

What is it?

No more sneaky microscopic writing!

No more fake lie detectors!

No more irresistibly beautiful documents!

No more trying to fool me.

259

Milton gives me a sly smile. Clearly, he enjoyed being slightly Rex-like for a while.

Okay. It's a deal.

One other thing.

Yeah?

"You are, without a doubt, more like Danny Doogood than anyone I've ever met in my entire life. Danny would be proud to know you."

"Thanks," he says. "You're pretty darn Annabelle yourself."

If Milton and I were the kind of partners who hugged, we might have hugged. But we're not. So we don't.

That afternoon, I sort of try to halfway listen as Mr. Shine gives us spelling tips.

When spelling words like *believe* and *fierce*, and *siege*, which comes first, *I* or *E*?

Mr. Shine looks right at me. "Are you paying attention, Moxie?"

"Absolutely!" I say. But of course I am thinking about anything and everything but spelling.

I keep glancing over at Emily, happy and relieved that my

MISSING BEST FRIEND has finally been found.

It might be the greatest feeling in the whole entire world.

Mei Lee starts waving her hand like it just caught on FIRE!

Yes, Mei?

What's that on the floor?

Mr. Shine bends down and picks up an envelope that's lying next to the trash can.

Moxie, it looks like this is for you.

Mr. Shine walks over to my desk and hands me the envelope.

My name is on the front. There is no stamp or return address. But there is a purple squiggle.

I'm gripped with terror!

I'm filled with delight!

This could be a Squiggler trap! Or it could be a nice letter from someone who thinks I'm great!

Tammy Dublinger gives me a look that says, *For the love of Pete, are you going to open it?* Looking around the room, I see 23 other sets of eyes asking the same question.

"Go ahead, Moxie," says Mr. Shine. "I don't think we're going to be learning anything until you read your letter, anyhow."

Dear Moxie,

I want you to know how much I appreciate you. You are amazing. You are a remarkable person. You care so much. You try so hard. You have a heart the size of Jupiter. Try not to be so hard on yourself. Thank you for everything you do for Tiddlywhump Elementary.

— The person you'd least expect

I put my letter back into its envelope and just sit there for a moment, letting the words travel the distance between my brain and my heart.

CHAPTER 15: TROUBLING CONCLUSIONS

The final bell rings, and I rush to the front of the school, where Milton is waiting. I show him my letter.

"That's really nice," he says.

"Have a look at mine."

"You got one, too?"

"Yesterday."

"Why didn't you tell me?"

Milton gives me a look, and I suddenly remember that we haven't exactly been on speaking terms lately.

I read Milton's letter. It is full of things that *seem* really nice but obviously aren't.

> Milton—
> I want you to know how much I appreciate you. You are so smart. You are so nice. I like how you do math.
> — The person you'd least expect

"I'm worried about you," I say. "I'm worried about *both* of us. Now that we've been Squiggled, we could be victims of a diabolical scheme!"

"*What* diabolical scheme?"

"The Squiggler's secret plans to destroy Tiddlywhump and everything Eddie stands for!"

Have you been reading Annabelle Adams again?

Every morning, without fail, for at least 20 minutes and occasionally more.

I assume you're thinking about Volume 6: *Death by Envelope*?

I am!

I'm extremely pleased that Milton has done his homework.

It's a *book*!

An excellent book.

It's *imaginary*!

But extremely convincing!

Moxie!

Yes?

Read your letter.

I have read it probably 200 times.

Read it again.

I read it again. Gosh, it is so nice.

267

"Now ask yourself: does it seem as if a diabolical supervillain like 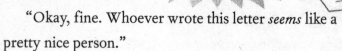 could have written it?"

"Okay, fine. Whoever wrote this letter *seems* like a pretty nice person."

Now read this one.

And this one.

Describe the type of person who would write them!

I do. The letters are full of compliments and kind thoughts and warm wishes.

I hate to admit it, but it does seem impossible that *any* of them could have been written by a criminal mastermind.

Instead, they're full of the sort of things that only someone as good and caring and thoughtful as my one true best friend, Emily Estevez, might say. But I do not mention this to Milton, because of course Emily is not the Squiggler. That would be ridiculous. Like a bulldog with a bow tie.

WHO YOU CALLIN' RIDICULOUS?

When we get home, we combine my big stack of letters with Milton's small stack of letters. While I sit on a stool and sip lemonade, Milton sorts them all into various piles in various rows, each of which clearly means something to him. I am full of questions, but whenever I ask one, Milton tells me not to interrupt. So I sit.

And watch.

And wait.

Eventually, he picks up one of the letters and walks over to my stool.

I've reached a troubling conclusion.

Oh?

This was from your pile, which is why I hadn't noticed it before.

He's holding up John's letter, the second one the Squiggler sent.

What about it?

Look along the top.

Along the top is a row of hearts.

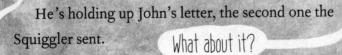

Now look at this.

Milton hands me a list of third graders with most of the names crossed out.

Okay. I see the same row of hearts at the top. But this isn't your handwriting. Who wrote it?

Milton looks GRIM.

My former partner,

he says.

When we were trying to narrow the list of suspects.

I'm struggling to understand what Milton is trying to tell me. I hold the two pieces of paper side by side.

"The hearts are the same," I say. "And the handwriting is definitely the same. Which means . . ."

Milton looks SICK TO HIS STOMACH.

The Squiggler is actually . . .

Don't say it!

Emily Estevez.

I'm too stunned to even gasp.

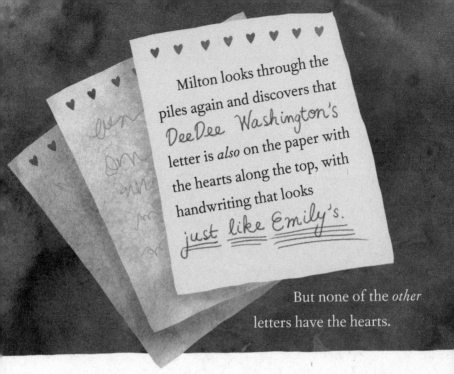

Milton looks through the piles again and discovers that *DeeDee Washington's* letter is *also* on the paper with the hearts along the top, with handwriting that looks *just like Emily's.*

But none of the *other* letters have the hearts.

And none of the *other* letters match Emily's handwriting.

NOPE

ISN'T HERS

NOT THIS ONE.

NOR THIS ONE

NOT EVEN CLOSE

NAH

DIFFERENT

UNALIKE

NOT A MATCH

NO

UH-UH

NEIN

I try to make sense of it all. Emily hired us to identify the Squiggler, but now we have reason to believe that she *herself* is the Squiggler. Which means she's been leading us on a wild-goose chase *this entire time*!

YOU CAN'T CATCH MEEEE!!

I find myself jumping to conclusions.

And so I give myself a talking-to.

The last time I thought Emily had done something dastardly, I ended up accusing her and regretting it. Perhaps there is a logical explanation. Even if I can't imagine what it could possibly be.

Milton takes out his markers and ruler and spends the next few hours making a fantastic diagram. There are circles representing the people who have gotten letters. Each one is connected with an arrow to another circle with a question mark inside.

It's amazing. And incredible. And so very . . . Milton.

"What does it mean?"

"Well, we know for sure that Emily sent letters to John and DeeDee."

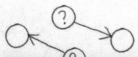
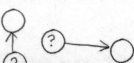

I take a closer look and see that John's and Dee-Dee's circles are connected to a circle with Emily's name inside.

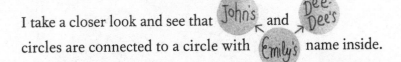

But who sent the rest of them?

There are so many question marks.

Was it Emily?

The answer to this question is very important to me.

"Well. It could have been Emily, using different kinds of paper and disguising her handwriting," says Milton.

"But . . . is it *possible* that it was someone else instead?"

"It is possible. I might even consider it likely."

"You mean . . . ?"

"Yes, I think there might be *more than one* Squiggler."

My mind **EXPLODES**

like a balloon
at a porcupine's
birthday party.

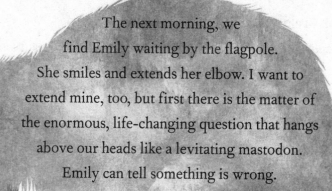

The next morning, we
find Emily waiting by the flagpole.
She smiles and extends her elbow. I want to
extend mine, too, but first there is the matter of
the enormous, life-changing question that hangs
above our heads like a levitating mastodon.
Emily can tell something is wrong.

What is it?

I cut to the chase.

We know the truth.

Emily looks panicked, and my heart collapses.

FETCH ME MY
SMELLING
SALTS!

"You *do*?"

"We *think* we do," says Milton. "But maybe you
can clear something up for us."

I take Emily's hands and look her
straight in the eye. I could be staring
into the eyes of a deranged criminal
or I could be sharing a pleasant
moment with my very best friend.

Are you . . . the Squiggler?

No! Of course I'm not!

My heart un-collapses. But Emily's face suggests there's more to the story.

And . . . well . . . yes. I *sort of* am! I mean . . . it's very complicated.

My heart collapses for the second time in less than thirty seconds.

"I think we'd better sit down," says Milton.

We find a bench. Emily looks like she just cut an onion. "I *did* send an anonymous letter to John," she says. "I just couldn't help myself. He's always so sad and unsure. I felt fantastic when I got my letter, and I wanted to make John feel that good, too."

"That was pretty nice of you," says Milton.

"It *was* nice," I say. "But why did you ask us to catch the Squiggler if the Squiggler is *you?*"

"*I'm not the Squiggler!*
The Squiggler is the person
who sent *my* letter to *me!*"

Milton pulls out DeeDee's
note and hands it to Emily.
"What about this?"

"Oh . . . right . . . erp! I just
couldn't help myself *a second time*," says
Emily on the edge of tears.

"DeeDee really needed a lift. She was so excited about
her purple socks and no one was paying attention. I'm sorry
I didn't tell you guys.
I've been feeling
terrible about it."

My best friend really needs a hug,
and I'd really like to give her one,
but we are in the middle of an
official interrogation, and
so I try to act professional
and keep asking
hard-hitting
questions.

276

Emily looks so sad that I decide she needs a friend more than the world needs a detective.

"I believe you," I say.

"Me too," says Milton. "Which means we still haven't caught the actual Squiggler."

I think of Annabelle Adams, Volume 55:

Copycatastrophe,

in which seven jewelry stores are robbed

on seven consecutive nights

WED	THURS	FRI	SAT	SUN	MON	TUE
10	11	12	13	14	15	16

by seven different criminals,

each of whom is inspired by sheer admiration of the previous evening's heist. Eventually, all the jewelry in town has been stolen, so Annabelle opens a fake jewelry store and waits in the fake safe for the eighth copycat with handcuffs and a knowing grin.

has a term for this. "Emily is what's known as a copycat," I say. "That is, someone who hears about a crime and decides to do the exact same thing, imitating as many details as possible."

"I want to point out that I don't consider myself a criminal," says Emily.

"Criminals never do," I say.

"What if there are *other* copycats?" asks Milton.

And if there are, how will we ever find out how many?

And who they are?

And which one sent that first letter to Emily?

The three of us sit there, not knowing what else to say. The case seems hopeless. Every time we answer a question, a new one pops up. Every time we think we get somewhere, it turns out we're actually further away.

278

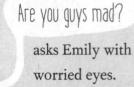

Are you guys mad?

asks Emily with worried eyes.

"Nope," says Milton.

"I couldn't be if I tried," I say. I know this is true, because I did try to be mad at Emily for a few minutes this morning and it didn't work. She's the type of person who simply can't stop herself from trying to make sad people feel better. Even if it means acting like a deranged criminal.

Now that we know who the Squiggler *isn't*, it's time to figure out who he—or she—actually *is*.

CHAPTER 16: I AM THE SQUIGGLER

Just like every other day, Mr. Shine sits on
the edge of his desk and asks us questions.

> Who can tell me something
> about ancient Egypt?

Tracy Dublinger raises
her hand. "Ancient Egypt was a
civilization that happened thousands of
years ago along the Nile River."

"That's right, Tracy. What else . . . ? Marita?"

"They built pyramids."

"They sure did. And they did other amazing things as
well. Who knows what else they did?"

Apparently, nobody knows.

"All right. How do you think they knew how
many blocks they'd need to build each
pyramid? Elliot?"

Elliot's got nothing.

"How about this . . . if the ancient Egyptians knew they wanted to build a pyramid that was 500 feet wide, and each block was 10 feet wide, how would they figure out how many blocks they needed?"

Something in Elliot clicks. "They had math?"

"Yes! And that's not all. How do you think we know so much about Egyptians today?"

"The Internet?"

"Partly, but if one ancient Egyptian had a really good day and he wanted to tell his friend who lived all the way on the other side of ancient Egypt all about it, what would he do?"

"No texting in ancient Egypt, right?"

"Right."

"Maybe he would . . . write his friend a letter?"

"Yes! Excellent. The ancient Egyptians had a system of writing with pictures called hieroglyphs."

Mr. Shine smiles. Elliot smiles. I start smiling myself. It's hopelessly contagious.

It suddenly occurs to me that as much as Mr. Shine knows about ancient civilizations, he might also know a thing or two about modern Squigglers.

"Yes, Moxie?"

"What if, for example, there had been a terrible *crime* in ancient Egypt?"

"What sort of crime?"

"Well . . . do you happen to know what people liked to eat in ancient Egypt?"

"BREAD, ONIONS, AND DRIED FISH."

"Well . . . let's suppose that someone kept leaving, um, dried fish . . . in other people's cupboards all over ancient Egypt, but nobody knew whether it was a nice, generous thing to do or whether it was just part of a dastardly conspiracy to destroy ancient Egypt and build an ancient shoe factory."

"Hmm . . . What makes
this dried fish so dangerous?"

"Nobody knows! It might just be normal
dried fish or might be dried fish that turns you
into a mindless zombie who can't do math."

"I see," says Mr. Shine. "What was your
question again?"

"How do you figure out who's leaving all
this dried fish all over the place? Especially if
you find some in your cupboard and you really
need to know whether or not it's safe to eat?"

Mr. Shine looks out at the class.

"Moxie is asking
a very interesting
question. If you
can't figure out who
is leaving dried fish
in your cupboard,
what do you do?"

Felipe is the first to raise his hand. "It probably smells pretty bad, right? You could just sniff around and see who smells like dried fish."

Mr. Shine smiles. "For the sake of discussion, let's assume the fish doesn't smell."

Emily chimes in. "I'd probably be so thankful for the dried fish that I'd go catch a fish and dry it out for someone else."

That Emily Estevez! Even in ancient Egypt, she's too generous for her own good.

"Thank you, Emily," says Mr. Shine. "Yes, Chaz?"

"I'd set up a webcam in the cupboard and catch the dried fish mummy in the act."

"What makes you think it's a mummy leaving the dried fish, Chaz?"

"Definitely a mummy," says Chaz. "Definitely."

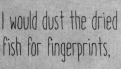

I would dust the dried fish for fingerprints,

says George.

I would use lasers!

says Jose. He does not explain what the lasers would do.

"These are all interesting ideas," says Mr. Shine. "Any others?"

Apparently, there are no other ideas.

"Well, did you get your answer, Moxie?"

"Maybe, but . . . I want to know what *you* would do, Mr. Shine."

He comes over and stands by my desk.

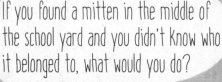

If you found a mitten in the middle of the school yard and you didn't know who it belonged to, what would you do?

"I'd ask the kids standing nearby if it belonged to any of them."

"Good thinking. Might that work with the dried fish? In ancient Egypt?"

"But how would you know who to ask?"

"Well, if I were in ancient Egypt, I'd line *everyone* up against the biggest pyramid and look them straight in the eye and ask whether or not they'd left dried fish in my cupboard."

"Everyone?"

"How else are you going to know for sure?"

"There were a lot of ancient Egyptians."

Yes, there were. Sometimes your ability to solve a problem depends on how hard you're willing to work for the solution. Actually, that's true most of the time.

Did that help?

"I think so," I say. But I'm still not sure.

I go over the other kids' ideas, but I can't see how 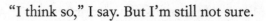 or are going to help us catch the Squiggler. But then I think of what Mr. Shine suggested, and it gives me an idea. An outrageous, shocking, perfect idea.

When recess begins, I know what must be done.

Skip Recess Helpers today,

I whisper to Emily on our way out of the classroom.

But—!

Trust me, it's important.

Emily looks at me with her enormous heart.

Okay, she says.

I have to go!

I say, squeezing her hand and sprinting out the door. And it's absolutely true. I have a world to save.

First I find Milton. He's on his way to our bench.

Not today.

Why not?

Today's the day we catch the Squiggler.

How?

Milton is excited.

"Do you still have that *EXTREMELY IRRITATING WHISTLE*?"

"Always," he says, pulling it out of his pocket.

Milton looks worried and excited and a little bit impatient as he follows me to the base of the jungle gym. "What's the plan?"

"I'm just going to ask."

"Who?"

"Everyone in ancient Egypt."

"*What?*"

I put one arm around Milton's shoulder and point my other at the school yard. "One of our fellow Tiddlywhumpians *has to* be the Squiggler, right?"

"Right."

"So I'm just going to ask."

"Who?"

"Everyone."

"When?"

"Right now!"

Milton is excited. "How?"

"Here's what I need you to do. When the time comes, keep your eye on the crowd and help me spot the Squiggler."

"When will the time come?"

"You'll know."

I climb and I climb, up to the very top of the jungle gym. I look across the school yard at my fellow students, all of whom are playing kickball and tetherball and freeze tag and chatting with one another without a care in the world.

I blow Milton's whistle until I run out of breath. It's a horrible sound. I'm glad when I run out of breath.

Everyone stops talking and shouting and playing and looks up at me in wonder.

Which is exactly what I'm going for. I raise my arms above my head like an explorer announcing her arrival on a brand-new planet. What I'm doing is strange and exciting. They all walk toward the jungle gym—the little kids, the big kids, the medium-sized kids, the teachers. Everyone.

When they're close enough to hear me, I begin to speak. I've never had trouble being loud when I need to. "Friends . . . as you know, these have been strange days at Tiddlywhump Elementary."

I look out at a sea of nodding heads.

"It all started when the world's most lovable fourth grader, Emily Estevez, received a mysterious letter in her mailbox. Because she wanted to know who sent it, Emily turned to me, Moxie McCoy, the single greatest detective in the history of Tiddlywhump Elem—"

Milton clears his throat really loudly.

"*And* my little brother, Milton, the *other* single greatest detective in the history of Tiddlywhump!"

There is a small amount of applause from a cluster of first graders near the seesaw.

"As you know, Emily's letter was followed by another. And then a whole lot more. Raise your hands if you've received a letter from the Squiggler!"

Pretty much everyone raises at least one hand. Some kids raise both.

"That's what I thought. And yet . . . does anyone know who the Squiggler is?"

I look around. The crowd is silent.

"Does anyone *want* to know who the Squiggler is?"

A loud cheer suggests that *everyone* wants to know.

"Exactly! We *all* want to know who you are, Squiggler! Some people say you are good and kind and generous. Others fear you plan to turn us all into terrible spellers! Whatever your aim, I challenge you to step forward and reveal yourself now!"

There is a great stretch of silence, as 146 sets of eyes look up at me. No one speaks. As far as I can tell, no one even blinks or breathes.

And so I decide to raise the stakes. "Squiggler, I challenge you in the name of *Tiddlywhump Elementary*!"

The air is electric. My cheeks burn. My fingertips tingle. Something is on the verge of happening. The Squiggler is about to crack. I just need to lay down my final card.

"Squiggler, I challenge you *in the name of our fearless mascot, Eddie the great horned owl,* and the timeless virtues of *courage, patience, and wisdom* for which he stands!"

There is a collective swell of indescribable excitement. Anything is possible.

And then, from somewhere in the middle of the crowd, I hear a voice. It is a voice I know. It is the voice I had been hoping for.

I am the Squiggler!

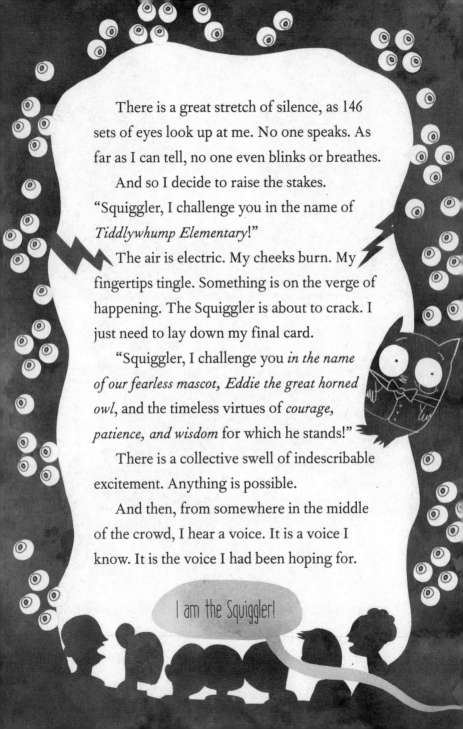

The crowd parts, and Tracy Dublinger is standing there with an awful, diabolical smirk on her face.

Once again, Tracy is the evil mastermind! I watch with excitement and anticipation, waiting for everyone to point and

BOO _and_ HiSS,

waiting for the authorities to come and take her away to a dark and distant place before she can command her brainwashed masses to reduce Tiddlywhump to a smoldering heap.

But something else happens instead. Something awful and unthinkable. Kids start crowding back around Tracy, cheering and thanking her and giving her enthusiastic high fives.

I look out into the crowd and see Emily. *She* is not crowding around Tracy. She looks . . . *mad.*

PIPING **HOT** MAD.

Before I can scramble down and give her a hug, Emily climbs up on top of the seesaw

and shouts in a voice that is clear and strong and true and even a little bit proud,

I AM THE SQUIGGLER!!

There is a collective **GASP** as every head turns in Emily's direction.

And then back at Tracy, who looks like a bush that just got pruned.

Everyone is trying to figure out what to do and who to believe when another voice cuts through the air.

I AM THE SQUIGGLER!!

It is Milton, standing on our bench and holding his hands in the air. My brother. My *partner*!

My brain goes off like a pan of popcorn kernels that just got hot enough to burst.

While everyone stands there in disbelief, another voice emerges from the most unexpected corner of the school yard.

I AM THE SQUIGGLER!!

Every single head turns in a different direction now, over to the tetherball pole, where Mr. Shine is smiling like the surface of the sun.

The shock is even bigger this time. A *teacher*, the *Squiggler*? How is it *possible*? But also *confusion*!!!!

How can Tracy and Emily and Milton and Mr. Shine *all* be the Squiggler?

It makes no sense!

But things are just getting started.

I lose track of who's talking. Enthusiastic confessions keep coming in waves, overlapping and jumbling together into one rolling ball of spectacular sound.

In the middle
of it all, Tracy Dublinger is
standing all alone, grumpy as a
soggy old duck whose feathers
aren't working.

Soon everyone is chanting,

I AM THE SQUIGGLER!!
I AM THE SQUIGGLER!!

Even *Tammy Dublinger*! At which point, it doesn't
make a scrap of sense for me to deny what is absolutely
true. After all, I wrote a letter. I drew a purple squiggle.
No matter that I sent that letter to myself. I am a part
of this enormous thing that's happening all around me.

And it feels AMAZING.

I wrap my ankles around the crossbars and lift my arms
like a queen marching over a mountain.

A cheer goes up from the crowd.
It might be the greatest moment
in the history of the world.

Emily is grinning like she just won a marathon. Milton is leaping in the air and giving everybody high fives.

Mr. Shine walks over to the base of the jungle gym and gives me the kind of smile that lets me know I've done something really good.

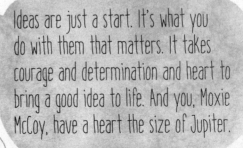

Did you find the answer to your question?

I absolutely did.

Well done.

It was your idea.

Ideas are just a start. It's what you do with them that matters. It takes courage and determination and heart to bring a good idea to life. And you, Moxie McCoy, have a heart the size of Jupiter.

301

I'm floating on a cloud of pure delight when my brain wraps itself around what Mr. Shine has just said.

"A heart the size of——?"

Mr. Shine gives me a great big wink.

"You mean——"

"As I said, I am the Squiggler."

"But when I asked, you said you *weren't!*"

"I wasn't the Squiggler yesterday. Today I am. People change. Isn't that wonderful?"

Mr. Shine smiles.

I smile.

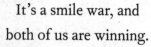

It's a smile war, and both of us are winning.

I look out at the school yard and think to myself that Annabelle would be proud.

As it turns out, I was entirely wrong. There is no diabolical scheme. The Squiggler is not a deranged criminal bent on making us sad. The Squiggler is actually a whole bunch of people trying to make one another happy.

As it turns out, Mr. Shine is not the Squiggler and Milton is not the Squiggler and Emily is not the Squiggler.

As it turns out, we *all* are.

CHAPTER 17: THE PERSON YOU'D LEAST EXPECT

Milton and Emily and I are sitting
together at lunch, trying to figure out
what to do next.

We've solved the mystery and
saved the day. We could just spend the rest of our lives
feeling proud of ourselves. But we still don't know who sent
that original letter to Emily.

And I really, really want to know.

What would Annabelle Adams say? I ask.

What would Danny Doogood recommend?

counters Milton.

"Annabelle always says the case isn't closed
until the jewels are back in the vault," I say.
"What does that have to do with our case?"
"Even though there are no *actual* jewels in this
mystery, the Squiggler did steal
something from Emily."
"What?"

"Her peace of mind," I say. "Until we figure out who sent that first letter, Emily won't be able to sleep at night."

"Actually, I've been sleeping just fine," says Emily.

"But I want you to sleep even *better*."

"That's nice of you."

"Danny Doogood often says that you can't solve a problem until you know the right question to ask," says Milton.

What does that have to do with our case?

We weren't asking the right question before.

What do you mean?

Before, we were trying to figure out who had *sent* the letters. But we should be asking, "Who did *you* send letters *to*? We have to work backward to find the original Squiggler."

And even though it's Danny's idea, I find myself agreeing with it.

Milton, Emily, and I spend the next few days talking to everyone we can, asking kids who they sent letters to. As it turns out, Milton was Squiggled by Dee Dee Washington, who was inspired to write him a letter when he said something nice about her purple socks.

Whenever we get a new piece of information, Milton adds it to his diagram. Eventually, there are just four question marks left.

So close.

And yet so far.

I think we've reached a dead end.

Not quite.

"What do you mean?" I ask. Something FISHY is happening. Milton looks GUILTY!

Instead of answering, he goes over to the diagram and replaces three of the question marks with his own name.

You didn't!

I did.

But why?

I just couldn't help myself. It felt so good.

I understand.

Me too,

I say, though I'm not entirely sure I mean it.

We gaze at the diagram together. Other than the original Squiggler, every question mark has been replaced with a name. Everyone is connected to everyone else.

"What's so great is that no one just *got* a letter," says Milton. "Everyone who got one also *sent* one to someone else."

"Well, *almost* everyone," says Emily. It sounds for a second like she's going to continue her thought, but then she stops herself and takes a bite of her apple instead.

I see what Emily is talking about. I'm the *almost*. I received a letter, but the only letter I sent was to myself.

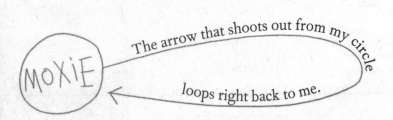

MOXIE

The arrow that shoots out from my circle loops right back to me.

But Milton and Emily aren't dwelling on that. As we stand there staring at the diagram, there's so much to feel good about. Emily puts her arm around my shoulder, and Milton takes my hand.

It's amazing.

It's beautiful.

It's incomplete.

"You're right," says Milton, shaking his head at the final question mark.

"Maybe it's just as complete as it's *supposed* to be," says Emily.

"Ridiculous!" I say. "The jewels are not yet back in the vault!"

"Maybe that's the point," says Emily. "Maybe it's better that we don't know who started this. Maybe that makes everything that's happened over the past few weeks a little more *Magical*."

Apparently, Emily doesn't understand that there is no room for magic in the mind of a detective. But she looks so happy that I don't have the heart to tell her so.

The next day in class, Mr. Shine is asking questions about the moon, and I notice that Tracy Dublinger seems slightly less miserable than usual. A few minutes later, she opens her binder to take out her homework, and I catch a glimpse of something in the pocket.

An envelope.

With her name written on the front.

And a purple squiggle.

My brain splits in two.

One half is trying really hard to figure out how in the world anyone could have come up with a single nice thing to write about Tracy Dublinger.

SRSLY?

But the other half is glad that, whatever kind words the letter contains, Tracy is getting the chance to read them.

YOU GO, GRL!

And then the first half chimes back in and makes an important point. Milton's amazing diagram is already

One afternoon a few weeks later, Milton and I ride the bus home with Emily again, only this time we have an actual note from Dad.

I've been wanting to pay a proper visit to Emily's

SLUG TERRARIUM.

There must be dozens of them inside, crawling every which way without a care in the world.

They're so beautiful.

I love them more than life itself.

You guys are weird, says Milton.

He is fiddling with Emily's alarm clock, trying to turn it into a mind-reading device.

There is a knock on the door, and one of Emily's dads comes in.

"Here you go, kiddo. Just found this in the mailbox. But the mail came an hour ago, so it wasn't the mailman who put it in there." He hands Emily an envelope. She looks at it and gasps.

Look! she says, pointing to the purple squiggle.

Impossible! says Milton.

Is this from–? says Emily.

I think it might be, I say.

The squiggle is in a different place than it was on Emily's original letter. Right above it is a note, written in black pen.

oops! It looks like I forgot to include the second page of my letter the last time I wrote.
— Glynnis

mily Estevez
24 Poplar Place

"What the——?" I say.

Emily's hands are shaking as she opens the envelope.

There's a letter inside. Or half of a letter, it seems.

"Do you have your original letter?" asks Milton.

"Right here," says Emily, pulling it out of her drawer.

"Put them side by side," I say.

Emily ———

I want you to know how much I appreciate you. You are good. You are kind. You are generous. You make this world a better place. I consider myself fortunate to know you. I hope you will always be true to yourself.

—The person you'd least expect

to lend a hand is often the person who can do the most good. So many fourth graders are so busy growing up that they don't come spend time with us older folks. Someone once told me that kindness and generosity of spirit are the most important qualities a person can have. You have both in spades.

Sincerely,
Glynnis Fitzgerald

P.S. The last time he was here, my great-grandson decided to decorate all my envelopes. I hope you don't mind.

We stand there for
a second, not saying a
thing. But it's extremely
loud inside my heart.

The person you'd least expect is named Glynnis.
The Squiggler is her great-grandson.

I look over at Emily. She's
crying the happy kind of tears.

Who is Glynnis?

Emily wipes her eyes. "A month or so ago, I went over
to the Tiddlywhump Home for Snappy Seniors and visited
with one of the women who lives there. I think she was
lonely. We spent about
an hour chatting about
how much she loves
gardening. I had already
forgotten about it."

"The jewels are back in the vault," I say.

I hold my hand up in the air in front of Milton. At first he blinks at it, as if trying to figure out what I'm trying to say. But then he gets it and smiles and raises his hand, too. We have a satisfying the kind that stings just enough to let the other person know you mean it.

Mom calls that night. She's finally done with her jungle trek and is back in cell phone range.

I tell her about Glynnis and the Squiggler.

"Here's the thing," says Mom. I can tell she's about to say something really wise, so I listen even more carefully than usual.

"Individual people do strange and wonderful things all the time.

Usually the wonderful thing happens and people get excited for a while

and then everything goes back to how it was.

But every once in a while, if we're really lucky, a *second* person comes along and has the courage and imagination to do the wonderful thing, too.

And then, suddenly, it's so much easier for a third and fourth person to join in."

"And then a whole bunch more people?"

"Exactly," says Mom. "And that's when *truly* remarkable things can happen."

I think about that. It has been a truly remarkable few weeks at Tiddlywhump.

"Glynnis did a nice thing," says Mom. "But Emily is the one who turned it into something fantastic. Emily is the real Squiggler. That's a friend I'd try to keep."

"She's the absolute best," I say.

"I love you," says Mom.

I say it back.

Afterward, Dad and Milton and I play eleven rounds of

which is a card game we made up and no one but my family understands because it has 37 rules that change whenever we feel like it.

Hey,

says Dad as we're cleaning up the cards.

Yeah?

Thanks for saving the world.

I couldn't have done it without Milton.

And Milton couldn't have done it without *you*.

I try not to smile but do anyway, and then I say good night and go to my desk and take out a piece of paper and a black pen. And a purple marker.

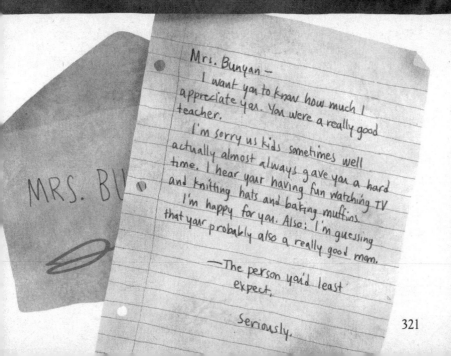

Dear Glynnis —
I want you to know how much
I appreciate you. Thanks to
you our entire school has
been nice to one another for
about a month which is pretty
much a miracle.
  I'd tell you my name but I
think its kind of better if I don't.

          Thanks for everything
          — The person you'd least
              expect

'LYNNIS

I seal the envelope and make a purple squiggle on the outside.

And then I take out another piece of paper.

Mrs. Bunyan —
  I want you to know how much I
appreciate you. You were a really good
teacher.
  I'm sorry us kids sometimes well
actually almost always gave you a hard
time. I hear your having fun watching TV
and knitting hats and baking muffins
I'm happy for you. Also: I'm guessing
that your probably also a really good mom.

          — The person you'd least
              expect.

          Seriously.

MRS. BU

321

I bring my letters down to breakfast the next morning.
Milton is already there, building something with his box
of parts.

What is it?

A time machine.

One that will actually work?

Hard to say. I'm just getting started.

Well, that could be pretty useful. Please keep me up to date.

I will.

We both sit there for a minute, eating, thinking, imagining.

What are those?

It's Milton's turn to wonder.

Letters.

For who?

I'd rather not say. Not because I don't want to tell
you, but because I think that's kind of the point.

"Squiggler letters?"

"Yep."

"I understand," he says, smiling just a little.

Milton attaches one end of a wire to a lightbulb
and the other end to a tiny battery. The bulb comes on.

"Nice job," I say.

"Thanks," he says. After a while, he continues, "If I
don't know who you're giving those letters to, how can I add
them to the diagram?"

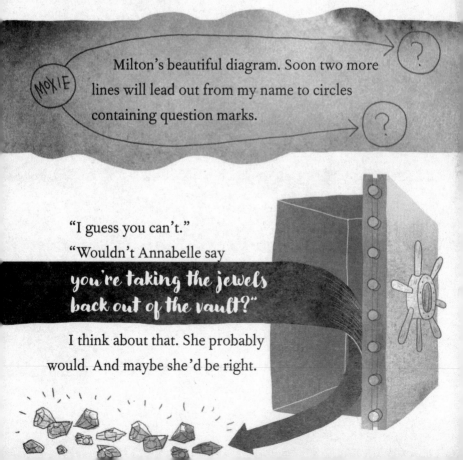

MOXIE

Milton's beautiful diagram. Soon two more
lines will lead out from my name to circles
containing question marks.

"I guess you can't."

"Wouldn't Annabelle say
you're taking the jewels
back out of the vault?"

I think about that. She probably
would. And maybe she'd be right.

"If Annabelle were here, I'd tell her that I absolutely am. On purpose. And I bet she'd say that sometimes right and wrong are absolutely backward from what you first thought."

Milton smiles as if I've said something really wise.

"You want to know what Danny Doogood would say?"

I really don't, but Milton clearly wants to tell me. "What?"

That our number one job each day is making the world at least a little bit better than we found it when we got up that morning.

It's hard to argue with Danny's intentions. It's his way of talking about them that I find a little hard to take.

"That Danny," I say, shaking my head. "I have to admit, he does make a good point every once in a while."

I pick up my letters and take my bowl to the sink. I give Milton a pat on the shoulder as I walk by his chair.

I get on my bike and head out. I have mailboxes to find.
And mysteries to create.

And precious jewels to leave out in the open, where anyone can see them shine.

BE A SQUIGGLER

The world is much better when people are kind and appreciative. Here's how to make your own Squiggler letter.

Supplies: envelope, piece of paper, pen, purple marker

1) Take out a piece of paper and write "Dear _____,"

2) Start by saying why you're writing the letter. For example:

   a. I am writing with exciting news.
   b. You probably have no idea how great you are.
   c. I want to let you know how much I appreciate you.

3) Say a few nice things about the person. Such as:

   a. What you like about them
   b. A nice thing that you know they did
   c. How they make you feel

4) Sign the letter with something other than your name. A few ideas include:

   a. A friend
   b. Your secret admirer
   c. The person you'd least expect

5) Make a purple squiggle on an envelope, put the letter inside, and then hide it somewhere the person will find it. Such as:

   a. In their lunchbox
   b. In their desk
   c. In their mailbox (but first make sure they are not watching from the roof!)

Or, if you want to download a Squiggler letter that's all set up for you, go to: realmccoysbook.com/squiggler-letter

But whatever you do, SQUIGGLE SOMEONE. I promise, you'll thank me!

WHO WE ARE
(AND HOW WE GOT THE IDEA FOR THIS BOOK)

HELLO!

We are Matthew Swanson and Robbi Behr. We are married and have four kids and drive a tired blue minivan.

In the winter, spring, and fall, we live and make books with Robbi's pictures and Matthew's words in the hayloft of an old barn on the Eastern Shore of Maryland.

In the summer, we live in a little red house on the Alaskan tundra, where we catch sockeye salmon and drive rickety pickup trucks and build elaborate forts among the alders.

Once upon a time, our Maryland doorbell rang, and when we went to see who it was, we found a lime-green coffee mug with a bow on the handle and a beautiful sunflower inside. We were excited, of course. We wanted to know who had done such a generous thing.

When we checked the card, it said this:

A small gift to brighten your day.
— Chester York

But we didn't know anyone named Chester York. And neither did anyone we asked. The next day, we heard that other people in town had gotten flowers from Chester York, too. But no one seemed to know who he was. For days and days, our entire town was electric with excitement and mystery.

Who is Chester York?

Why is he doing this?

What will happen next?

What happened next is that everyone was very kind and friendly and just a little more patient with one another. Because wherever you went, anyone you ran into might have been good old Chester York.

That was many years ago.

Matthew still drinks his morning coffee from the lime-green mug. But we still don't know who sent it.

Which is to say, the jewels are not yet back in the vault. And we hope they never will be.

To get on our mailing list, browse our other books, find our blog, or schedule us to speak at (or Skype with) your conference, library, or school, visit us at

WWW.ROBBIANDMATTHEW.COM

Thanks for reading!

Matthew & Robbi

MOXIE'S DICTIONARY

I love words. There are more of them than I could possibly ever learn or remember. But here are a few that I recently had to look up, just in case you're curious.

ARTICLES OF INCORPORATION: The fancy papers you sign when you're starting a new business. They don't have to be printed on an irresistibly beautiful certificate with a blue border and a gold seal, but it sure helps.

BRAINWASH: A diabolical method of repeatedly telling you what to believe that is so powerful it makes you forget everything you know and believe and love, even your cat, if you have one, which I don't. Does not involve soap.

BYLAW: A rule made by a company or legendary detective agency. Also: something sneaky little brothers sneak into fancy documents so that you don't actually know what you're agreeing to.

CHITCHAT: The kind of talking you do when you need to pass the time but don't really have anything to say.

COCKAMAMIE: A thing you might say about something that is ridiculous or unlikely, such as Tracy Dublinger writing a letter full of nice things about me.

CONUNDRUM: A confusing and difficult problem or question, such as how to feel about a bowl of avocado soup.

COPYCAT: Someone who imitates someone else, whether it's wearing the same kind of hat or robbing the same candy store. Copycats are very good at playing Simon Says.

DANNY DOOGOOD: Ugh!

DIPLOMA: A piece of paper you get when you finish college and are now allowed to be a principal, entomologist, or professional ninja. It is often irresistibly beautiful.

EUREKA: A word that you say when you make a sudden great discovery, such as you just figured out the identity of a kidnapping Squiggler. It's based on a word from ancient Greece, which is not so far away from ancient Egypt, where they had math and writing and ate dried fish.

GNOMISH: Like a gnome. Which is a person who is rather small. Like my brother. If you have a dictionary, go look up the word *gnomish*, and you'll probably see a picture of Milton. And if you don't, maybe you should draw one.

HAVOC: Widespread destruction, such as what happens to a bowl of guacamole when I'm near it. People who run amok often cause havoc.

IN SPADES: Weirdly, this phrase has nothing to do with tiny shovels or a pack of playing cards, and instead means that you have a lot of something—even if the something you have a lot of is tiny shovels.

JOHN HANCOCK: John Hancock wrote his name so huge and fancy on the Declaration of Independence that his name is now another way of referring to a signature. As in, I think I'll just put my John Hancock on this irresistibly beautiful document with the wavy blue border and the shiny gold seal.

NEWFOUNDLAND: A large island off the eastern coast of Canada. Also the breed of an enormous and very friendly dog named Mike owned by my crazy uncle Vern.

PAMPAS: A large, flat part of Argentina with no trees. Also home to many grazing cows. Also a great place to go sulk when you're feeling discouraged.

PRO BONO: It has nothing to do with being a pro, which I am, and nothing to do with bones, which I have more than 200 of, and instead means doing something for free, which I do when Milton makes me. Pro bono is Latin, which is a language that nobody speaks anymore but Principal Jones probably studied in college.

RUBBISH: Something I say to let someone know I think whatever they said is ridiculous, such as when Tracy's handshake is better than mine. Also, another word for garbage or trash.

RUN AMOK: To behave uncontrollably and disruptively. The teachers try to keep us from running amok at recess. But we sometimes do it anyway.

SMOG IN THE NOGGIN: This is an old-fashioned phrase from the 1950s, which is when my grandma was a little girl. Smog is a mixture of smoke and fog. A noggin is your brain. If you have smoke and fog in your brain, it doesn't do a very good job of remembering things.

SMOKE SCREEN: Something you use to make it seem like you're doing something else. There is no actual smoke involved—unless Tracy Dublinger's smoke screen was lighting a campfire and roasting marshmallows to make it seem like she wasn't just sitting there, plotting her next dastardly scheme.

SQUIGGLER: Someone who makes a squiggle. Which means you might be a Squiggler. Along with most three-year-olds.

TOOTHLESS EELS: Best avoided at all costs.

READ THE REST OF MY (EVER-EXPANDING) DICTIONARY AT REALMCCOYSBOOK.COM/MOXIES-DICTIONARY

GO FISH

MATTHEW SWANSON AND ROBBI BEHR

What did you want to be when you grew up?
Robbi Behr: I wanted to be an explorer who sailed in a big ship across the ocean and had a sword and tramped around in the jungle.

Matthew Swanson: What did you want to discover?

RB: *New worlds!* I figured they were everywhere. For example, I thought that Ohio was still a mostly wild and undiscovered territory.

MS: My ambitions were less grand. I wanted to be an actor, then a poet, then a singer-songwriter.

RB: What's less grand than being a poet?!

MS: Good point. I could have been the poet who wrote about your conquest of Ohio.

What were your hobbies as a kid? What are your hobbies now?
RB: I liked to read. I liked to draw. I liked to play video games. I guess that's pretty standard boring stuff.

MS: Are you saying that you were a standard, boring kid?

RB: No, no. There's no such thing, Matthew! All children are sparkling wonders.

MS: Are you saying that *you* were a sparkling wonder?

RB: That is exactly what I am saying. And now I am a somewhat larger wonder who continues to sparkle. What was *your* hobby?

MS: When I was little, I liked to have long conversations with my Legos, and when I got a bit older, I liked to write heroic couplets, which was part of my poet plan.

RB: What is your hobby now?

MS: Trying not to burn myself on the red-hot heat of Robbi's self-confidence.

RB: Good luck with that.

Where do you write your books?

MS: I write my books in a long, tall, narrow room that used to be a storage closet but is now quite magnificent.

RB: Come on, let's be honest here: that's actually a fairly recent development. You haven't actually *written* any books in the magnificent closet yet, have you?

MS: I've *edited* several books in the magnificent closet. Where do you write *your* books, Robbi?

RB: I don't write any books! I wake up in the middle of the night and tell Matthew my fabulous ideas, and he turns them into books. I write them in Matthew's head, and he does all the work!

MS: This is also how Robbi folds the laundry and does the dishes.

What advice do you wish someone had given you when you were younger?

RB: Not to worry about it.

MS: About what?

RB: About anything.

MS: Tell these kids one specific thing that they shouldn't worry about.

RB: Don't worry about what other people think.

MS: That's really good advice. I finally learned it when I was forty-three, but I wish I'd learned it when I was a kid. Because it might be the secret to everything.

If you could travel in time, where would you go, and what would you do?

RB: Does the future count? Wait, I don't want to go to the future, actually. Never mind.

MS: This is what is known as Robbi having a conversation with herself.

RB: Actually, I would probably go back in time to when Ohio was still wild and do my exploring.

MS: I would go back in time to the other night right before Robbi woke me up and started writing a book inside my head and see if I could convince her to let me sleep instead.

RB: I would not let you sleep. I would do it again. You should definitely use your time travel more wisely.

MS: Then I would go back and try to convince twelve-year-old Matthew not to care what other people think.

RB: I wish I could give twelve-year-old Matthew a big hug.

MS: Forty-four-year-old Matthew appreciates that.

Do you ever get writer's block? If so, what do you do to get back on track?

MS: I never, ever, ever, ever get writer's block.

RB: Matthew's like a fire hydrant. He's an unrelenting barrage of stories and ideas that I eventually have to illustrate. I really wish he would get writer's block every once in a while.

MS: I have four thousand ideas that I want to write all at once.

RB: The only time Matthew gets writer's block is when his hands get cramped and it hurts too much to type.

MS: But to get over actual writer's block, you just have to follow Robbi's advice! Don't worry about what other people think.

RB: Don't even worry about what *you* think.

MS: Exactly! Nobody's first draft is perfect, or even close. Just write and write and make it better later. You can't improve the stories you never write in the first place.

What would your readers be most surprised to learn about you?

RB: [After a long, conspicuous pause]. That I was a great big loser in middle school?

MS: If that is surprising, then I will say that I was *also* a great big loser in middle school. But I think these kids all just *assume* that you and I were great big losers in middle school.

RB: But then one day Matthew turned forty-three and stopped caring what people think and turned back into a sparkling wonder.

MS: What was I in the meantime?

RB: A sparkling wonder who just didn't know it yet.

MS: So what you're saying is . . .

RB: We are all always sparkling wonders, no matter what anyone else thinks.

What would you do if you ever stopped drawing or writing?

RB: If I ever stopped drawing, I'd be fine. I'd probably spend all my time eating tons of ice cream and watching TV. How about you?

MS: If I ever stopped writing, I would assume that something had gone terribly wrong, like that I had been abducted by aliens and that the actual me was now living on some other planet.

RB: I would make the same assumption. If Matthew ever stopped writing, I would head directly to outer space to try to get him back.

MS: Alternately, you could sit around and play a lot of video games with whoever the aliens had replaced me with?

RB: Hmm. You're right, that actually sounds way better.

MS: So much for your interest in exploration.

RB: Outer space doesn't hold a candle to Ohio.

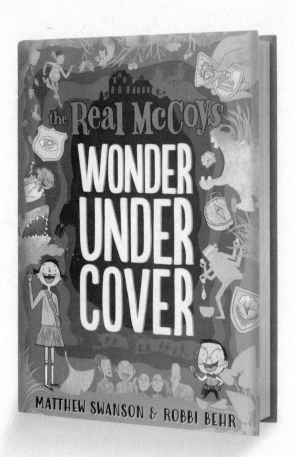

the Real McCoys

WONDER
UNDER
COVER

MATTHEW SWANSON & ROBBI BEHR

CHAPTER 1: DUBLINGER DISCORD

The name's Moxie. Moxie McCoy.

The world's greatest fourth-grade detective, at your service.

Here I am, 20 minutes before school starts, standing behind an extremely large bush.

WHY?

Because Emily Estevez, my very best friend in the whole entire world, asked me to.

It is a sneaky place to stand, and I like it.

Emily appears with a look that means she has terrible news or has recently had too much

"What did you have for breakfast?" I ask.

"Toast and jam."

"What's the bad news?"

"The truth is, I have very *good* news." But Emily says *good* the way a doctor says, *"Don't worry—this won't hurt a bit,"* right before jamming a

NEEDLE

into your arm. "Please try to keep an open mind," Emily says.

"I always do!"

"You sometimes don't."

I am tempted to feel wounded, but since I am talking to Emily, good as cheesecake, pure as water from the door of the refrigerator, I decide to keep an open mind. Emily has never led me astray.

I will try.

Good. The truth is, I have a case for you. But the name of your new client might . . . surprise you.

I have traveled the wide world. I have been to New Jersey. Which is to say, *nothing* surprises me.

Emily glances over my shoulder and gives a nod. I turn and see one unlovable Dublinger lurking behind a different bush nearby.

The Dublinger twins, Tammy and Tracy, are my sworn enemies.

Tracy is QUEEN OF THINGS THAT ARE AWFUL AND IRRITATING, and Tammy is the jester in her court.

At the moment, I can't tell which Dublinger I'm looking at, because they have

similar sneers

and identical noses

and always wear matching accessories.

The Dublinger approaches. I am preparing to say

 or  or

But Emily speaks first. "Hello, Tammy. Moxie has agreed to hear about your case and . . . *to keep an open mind*."

Hello, Tammy, I say with about as much pleasure as I might get from kissing a clam.

I wonder whether this is one of those times when it's okay to kick your best friend in the shin.

Tammy gnaws at the center of my soul with her beady blue termite-teeth eyes.

What seems to be the problem?

asks Milton, surprising me a little.

If I forgot to mention that my puny little brother, Milton, has been standing beside me this whole time, it's because he's so short that it almost hurts my neck to look down that far.

Milton fancies himself a detective, and technically we're partners, so I let him tag along when I'm working on cases. He sometimes says useful things. But mostly he collects dust and resembles a miniature accountant.

"Well?" I ask, tapping my foot to make perfectly clear how little patience I have left.

"It's better if I show you," says Tammy, who looks as if she'd rather tickle a triceratops than talk to me.

She pulls back her coat and reveals . . . her

WONDER SCOUTS SASH.

Ugh, I say before I can stop myself. And then, even though I could definitely stop myself, I say it again.

UGH.

The Wonder Scouts is a group of girls who think they are better than every other person on the planet. They wear blue sashes loaded with

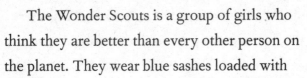

MEANINGLESS BADGES.

They spend at least two hours a day combing their hair. They meet three times a week to come up with new ways to be awful.

They have always made me think of Annabelle Adams, Girl Detective, Volume 23:

Not-So-Nice Guys,

in which a group of seemingly pleasant and charitable citizens turns out to be a renegade band of no-good swindlers who help little old ladies cross the street but then steal their purses and use the money to send fragile toys filled with glitter to unsuspecting toddlers.

But despite all that is wrong with the Wonder Scouts,
I can't help but be enchanted by Tammy's blue sash.
It is a magnificent mosaic of colorful patches, each a

delicately embroidered

reminder of accomplishment.

"So . . ." says Milton, trying to get us
back on track, "what seems to be the *problem*?"
Tammy Dublinger points to the one empty
spot on her sash.

the
MASTER
BAKER
BADGE

It's the last one I need to become the first Wonder Scout
to get all twenty badges. And I can't seem to do it.

"Nobody's perfect," says Milton in a comforting way.
"I am!" says Tammy in an irritating way.

Apparently not,

I say, looking at Tammy the way
you look at a swarm of gnats
before pulling out your bug spray.

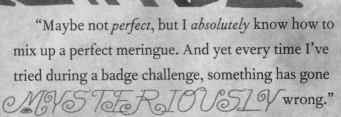

"Maybe not *perfect*, but I *absolutely* know how to mix up a perfect meringue. And yet every time I've tried during a badge challenge, something has gone MYSTERIOUSLY wrong."

"Do you want us to teach you how to make meringue?" asks Milton. "I might be able to find a recipe online."

"NO!" says Tammy. "I make *perfect* meringue at home. The only thing standing between me and the Master Baker badge is Tracy. I know she is sabotaging me. I just don't know how."

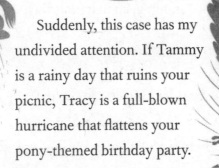

Suddenly, this case has my undivided attention. If Tammy is a rainy day that ruins your picnic, Tracy is a full-blown hurricane that flattens your pony-themed birthday party.

One Dublinger is hiring me to bring about the downfall of the other. This is the most wonderful thing since the invention of the book.

"I got my nineteenth badge a *month* ago. At that point, Tracy had only *fourteen*. Now she has nineteen badges, too. Now *she* could become the first Wonder Scout to get all twenty badges! Which would be *unacceptable!*" Tammy is getting pretty worked up. It's really kind of wonderful.

"What, exactly, do you want us to do?" I ask.

"Figure out what Tracy is doing to keep me from winning this badge. Expose her as the sneaky, lying cheater she is!" Tammy pulls a dollar from her pocket. "Will you take my case?" she asks, suddenly reluctant, as if asking a giraffe to lick her earlobe.

Milton and I lock eyes.

The challenge is clear, but the answer is *Oh heck yes*. We've been looking for the next big case. And this one is the Real McCoy.